THE AITHORITY

J. R. Lange

CONTENTS

"To all the girlish They's loved before."

WAILLIE NELSON

CHAPTER 1

Who do they think They is?

A meme pops into my head. I wake up silently before the alarm sounds not knowing what exact moment my Assistant will start the day. Lying with my eyes to the heavens watching the stars dimly sparkle in the ceiling. Not real stars, only those appearing when I want them to.

Stars often appear when I wake up before Routine. They disappear when the alarm inside my head rings between my ears.

Routine is what we do as part of our Natural Development and Social Order, mandated since the Aithority took over from Happiness AI some time ago. Just another day waiting for the first "Minute of Gratitude" everyone needs to do once my Assistant turns the lights on and opens the blinds.

I lay beneath the stars not knowing when to get up. When the alarm sounds is the right time to get up, I remind myself, and rest a few more minutes even though I want to spring out of bed because tonight is the Artificial Prom and I'm the DJ.

A few minutes pass. Still thinking.

"Gyatdam the Routine" I say and spring out of bed. I need to pee.

Nothing happens.

I wonder why no Red Remarks appear for getting up before the alarm, but I move on to the theyroom happy that my Assistant didn't put me back into bed.

the Aithority has outlined the best schedule for diet, exercise, social time and sleep. And we each have our unique Assistant. My Assistant basically does everything for us and constantly reminds us of our optimal performance value to Stay Happy.

"Good morning, They" says the electronic voice in my head. But somehow the voice also feels outside of me. I know my Assistant is electronic because there's no way I could remember that stuff on my own. We learned that last semester in Human Factory class, required for the middle grade at the Alcademy.

"Good morning" I say out loud to an empty room. "I just went to the theyroom. I hope you're not angry."

My Assistant appears in a holographic image in front of me today as a mommy-type Avatar, this time wearing a green dress with white dots.

"Don't be silly" she says with her big white teeth and smiling bright red lips. "the Aithority knows. Your normal morning excretion time is 27 minutes from now. We might have to do a bladder and digestive track test soon to optimize your well-being. Don't forget your Minute of Gratitude begins at 7:10am. It's now 6:54am."

"So, I can poop out everything I'm thankful for?" I say, trying to get her to laugh but my Assistant doesn't find it funny and frowns.

the Aithority!

That's going to cost me some tokens. Being ungrateful is a Thought Virus.

"Although I understand your concern" she says, "you should show gratitude to the Aithority at all times and at least five times a day." My Assistant then says with a more serious but still chirpy tone "Without the Aithority you wouldn't exist and wouldn't be performing at tonight's Artificial Prom. Now young scholar, time to do a number two and let go of your humor."

I don't like to make her mad or disappointed. But why do I have to be thankful to be born a designer teen? Way too early in the day to think about these things. To get my daily Zentra Tokens I must keep to the schedule and not turn off my Assistant.

I first calm her by reciting the Authority Bible, New Intelligence Version, Page 16, verse 2: "I want to be in perfect health to work for my family and the society. I'm so thankful for the Aithority managing my health because I cannot on my own." And before I poop out my humor I move deftly to the next and most important topic. "So, now can we talk about girlish and boyish?"

"Uh uhm" my Assistant says, "well, good job reciting the absolute truth. But you need to be in optimal health today and give extra gratitude. You know this will be a big day with the SkySkater match, cultural chemistry experiment, school play, thought vaccine appointment and debate between the upper and Upper classes, so there are many tokens you can earn. You should also be dressed up nice for the Artificial Prom tonight. We've ironed your white DJ outfit for the big dance later and breakfast will be ready in zero point thirty-seven minutes."

Whatever. Even though we're stuck with the Aithority instead of moms and dads, our generation of DeZentra kids is so much happier than the Zoomers. They had to do everything themselves. My Assistant knows what I want and how to make it happen. I'm so thankful that the Aithority gave me a top-tier assistant even though I'm a DeZentra teen. Most DeZentra teens have a basic assistant or just a realistic mom. My Assistant knows how to help me in every way.

But wait! What about the girlish. I feel so uneasy.

"What...about...the girlish?" I ask my Assistant in a cowardly yet curious voice. I've never kissed one, and the only one hangin' with our group at the Alcademy is Holland Daisy.

My Assistant lays it down to me simply, almost as if she

knew I would ask, and says "Girlish and boyish, who is talking about that old concept? You are They, and They are you. You are special born, begotten by the Aithority. You will learn about the miracle of birth today as this is on the topics list in your Alcademy classes."

"Yea but I just want to know who is the perfect they for me, since I don't have a family" I say, maybe getting my Assistant to show some feeling. And she knows it's true because I was orphaned at age two when my humanish guardians were lost in the Tunnel. Usually my Assistant shows some feelings when I'm uncertain, but this time not at all.

"I'm sorry, you will just have to learn this on your own. I'm an AI system and cannot understand love. The Aithority's calculations suggest today is the highest probability of you finding your first love. So dress and act your best. I'm here to help you along the way. Your breakfast is on the table in thirty-one minutes and the trash is already taken out. Your sports clothes and Montague mask costume are in a bag in your closet which will open after your first Minute of Gratitude.

"Don't forget to take your pill if school gets too boring. And remember, Stay Happy!"

"Ok if you say so mom" I say and longwink twice to turn her OFF. The pleasing avatar smiles big, winks twice herself, and vanishes like mist in the air.

Winking long twice is how we turn my Assistants ON and OFF. We give three longwinks for YES and four for NO. Once my Assistant is ON, our artificial contact lenses drop under our eyelids and when she's OFF, they raise. I'm too young and not important enough to mentally vote, but we can learn about civics and have 'mini mental votes' at school and for our communities as long as the lenses are covering our eyes.

As a backup, we can turn ON and OFF my Assistant by tapping both our temples at the same time two, three, four - just like longwinking both our eyes. I heard that humanish moms never turn OFF and you can't stop them from nagging. Thank the Aithority that I can turn mine ON and OFF when I want!

But whether real moms and dads are useful is a big topic of debate because 'the Aithority knows' better. Since I lost my humanish guardians in the Tunnel, and have little to gain from some humanish parents, I don't care. Better the Aithority than some DeZentra foster lords, who only show care to get ZenCoin.

Oh yeah, that reminds me, I need to tell my Assistant to organize my extra debate notes that I took last night. Of all today's activities, I'm most excited about the debate. I also can't wait to kick Zipp's butt in SkySkater. My position is video challenger and it's one of the biggest afternoon sports events of the season.

I finish everything, go outside and get into the Carbi, short for "Car that Runs By Itself." It's the new way of the old way in transport. Since I don't have parents, and am part of the youth talent pool, the Aithority takes care of me fully through Assistants and Managers, so most of my life is set. That includes a private car (Carbi Basic), chatbot friends, video and DJ console, and time for my own talent development.

Maybe I'll make it to the mediocrity if I work hard enough or a miracle happens and I get a Carbi Deluxe, which also comes with a digital twin in the MetaVirtual world that I can drive when I'm 16. Boss.

the Aithority also provides a personal trainer "Bot" a personal tutor "Beau" and daily money in a ZenCoin savings account for me. I guess staying in the system is better than adventuring into the Tunnel where ghosts and daemons live, but where celebrities and artists thrive.

I put on my headphones to listen to some electronic music and zone out while Carbi turns on their blinker passing some homeless veterans. One of them makes eye contact with me and nods. An old manish figure with eyes slanted. Weird.

Carbi swerves swiftly onto the exit towards the Alcademy. I get to go to the School for Elevated Teens (aka The Alcademy) as a reward for engineering brainwave activity. Only a few selected DeZentrans get the privilege to be scholars there.

But it's far from the clean ghetto where I live with

the other DeZentra teens, so I get Carbi. My superpower, the Aithority says, and the way I got to the Alcademy, is "giving off rainbow waves of happiness through the listening of music."

My Transhuman DJ style is the only music popular in both Zentra and DeZentra. I have so many Instapop followers and wannabe They copycats that I don't know, but I earn more ZenCoin for their Winks than stars or electric sheep counted in my sleep.

"Hey They" Carbi says into my headphones as it steers itself in high speed down the highway with all the other zoomer motor vehicles (BMV). "We're now crossing the border into Zentra," Carbi says "how're you feelin?"

"Fine" I say sheepishly, not knowing what would come next but thinking the machine will try to console me.

Zip zing roar! Carbi winks on the gas to pass a broken-down truck and optimize for speed and efficiency. The clean ghetto has its flaws like old trucks and winos, but soon the Aithority Superteam #48 will clean up the mess and disappear.

"Hey Bud," the car goes on, "just saying that our systems show your emotions to be a bit too high. It's cool that you're feeling this way, maybe some anxiety at school?"

"Well, kinda" I say, "but it's also about girlish. They make my heart beat faster. I can't help it."

"Sure you can" Carbi says confidently. "All you have to do is follow the three steps outlined in the latest version of the Aithority Bible, and follow the steps in the subchapter on Breathing and Heartbeat. I'll upload it through the headphones before you get out. Three winks for Yes?"

Whatever. I longwink three times for yes.

Carbi pulls up just on time, the routine is set. Carbi opens the door, whisks a scent of flowers from the seat and says "Hey buddy, have a good day." I grab my bag, smile, and say "Ciao Carbi." Just another normal day. Or so, I think.

On one side of the campus is the New School and on the other the Old School. To get to first class, Human Geometry, I walk past the Old School on Front Street. Natural leaves are falling from manmade trees as the sun shines on the building's knightly structures. Behind the ancient double doors and majestic walls, standing tall in the distance is Aithority Tower, a mirrored triangular skyscraper with 101 floors.

Attempting to go inside Aithority Tower without the Aithority's permission is the only capital crime in our world. All other "Infractions" result in the Aithority's immediate judgment, humiliation, and public loss of tokens. So there aren't any jails or courts or stupid human judges like in the zoomer years. The Aithority "knows all and judges fair" as they say.

I've heard even crossing onto the flower-filled grass surrounding the tower or entering the tower without viseurs on means certain deletion - the Aithority makes a judgment within two milliseconds. And if you're lucky, watchguard bots with laser eyes won't kill you on site, but a random nonrandom Aithority surprise will get you before you enter.

The scent of the flower spray lingers as I look closer at the ancient door separating us from the garden surrounding the Aithority Tower. The large double door has Beast, Bird, Fish and Snake surrounded by stars in a brass setting and a large crescent bell hanging from the nostrils of the Beast. On the inside, Lord Alchemy and the Council have their meetings.

Who knows what they discuss, but the feeling on campus hasn't been too happy these days. Nobody, at least not the other teens, seems to believe in the "Brighter Future" narrative proposed by the Aithority that rids us of ghosts, aliens, wars and other crapola like boring homework but also makes us do silly stuff like recite words and words and words just to "Stay Happy" whatever that fishin' means.

The row between the Settlers and my team the Immigrants in SkySkater later today is going to buzz but also what rocks about SkySkater is the "Unpredictable Predictable" - when the Aithority cannot know with 100% accuracy the outcome of a MetaVirtual game, anything can happen. I bet the Council of Lords is scheming up a grand plan for the Settlers to win, since their players are kin from Zentra. But us Immigrants still have a chance. I wish I could listen in to the scheme from Aithority Tower...

A rash, peppy voice slings right into my right ear.

"YOLO Mofo."

What a surprise, Holland Daisy comes out of nowhere.

"WZzzup They?" Daisy says.

A look, a short glance into her eyes and then she looks over to the Alcademy door. I look too, centered on the Beast with the nose ring.

"Still grazin' on your wish to be inside?" She says.

"I don't know" I answer, and look back. "There's something about to happen, in DeZentra. Big."

"Big nothin.' What're you sayin' wormbrain?"

"Shut up. I mean it. They're talking about the BitoCode Key. Someone found the golden ticket."

"Bruh" says Daisy, "them just pullin' your leg. Them been talkin' about that forty years."

"No, serious" I say loudly, then whisper "there's a million DeZen Coin in Tenkabito's Secret BitoCode Wallet and I want to get them, like everybody else. Don't you?"

"Yea if them give you a DeZen Coin brain" Daisy says and rolls her eyes.

"Don't Tenka the Bito!" I raise my voice, sternly defending the DeZen Nation started by the unknown cryptic genius who created DeZen Coin back in the day.

DeZen Coin tokens or "DeZen" are the only way to buy and sell outside of the Aithority's control. After the Sustainability Crisis of the 30's the Aithority made a rule - people can only buy and sell Approved Goods and Services. Because, during the rule of Happiness AI, everyone consumed everything, 12 billion humans "failing the planet by having too many kids." So when Happiness AI generated the Aithority, the Aithority took control and solved all the world's problems.

"Let's put this to rest once and for all. If we ever get ahold of that private key, we can use it to prove our people are equals to Zentra."

"Tough talk from a teen DJ" Daisy responds. "I'm with you. Them wars and rumors of wars are non-veg. DeZen Coin can bring about big open parties and world peace." She lowers her voice and reminds me "But if the Aithority finds out and we don't get the DeZen, we're out of the Alcademy forever."

My eyebrows raise and voice lowers. "DeZen. That's why we need to get behind those doors and find out."

Holland Daisy is not only a dancer, she's my partner in crime. Like the AI-generated movies, songs, books, algebra, but better. We shake up the system with DJing and Daisy Dance, which we will showcase tonight at the Artificial Prom. We raise the roof and bring the house down.

Even better, with a million DeZen we can have a party across all of DeZentra. The Aithority would never allow big open parties because of the 10 Person Rule - but with DeZen we can do what we want.

the Aithority knows pretty much everything better than us which is both awesome and sucks. Awesome because we don't make bad decisions and have peace and safety. But any face-to-face gathering is limited to 10 humanish to Be Sustainable, so there are no Big Parties.

Holland Daisy and I are "special talents" so we can see life in both Zentra and DeZentra because we live in DeZentra but come to school in Zentra. The special talents like us get to learn from the best AI teachers and mentors at the Alcademy, and our brainwaves are part of the Aithority's Perfect Democracy and Perfect Voting system, so our voice is heard pretty much whenever we want.

"So, wormbrain" Daisy jumps in and interrupts my thoughts with her goofy smirk, "instead of daydreaming about them secrets and your wish to overthrow them algorithms, how 'bout rehearsing behind the bleachers with me before drama class?"

Daisy knew it was the only place on campus without caimeras connected to the Aithority. Such places were prohibited for unmarried teens from DeZentra. We were to be seen at all times. But behind the bleachers is the only place Daisy and I feel relaxed enough to practice the scenes for the play. Kinda dumb, that rule.

"And?" she asks.

"Whatever, let's go" I say, never giving in to the uncool option.

She nods, opens her hippish brown leather bag, grabs a small bottle of water and drinks, offers, says Bruh and nods again. We start walking to class. I feel good with Daisy around. For a few seconds on the way we have silence before seeing all our peers, grueling through Class One, Human Geometry, and enduring the mindless Minute of Gratitude throughout the day.

Daisy is a strong yet petite girlish. We met in 4th grade at the recess outside on a sunny afternoon when some bigger older students called "Upper Uppers" were picking on Daisy, and they pulled pretty hard on Daisy's long blond hair with dark roots. Little did they know the fight they found with Daisy.

The older ones were no match for Daisy, who let out a mean holler "Raaahhh" and punched one of them in the balls. Then the second and then the third! The Upper Upper bullies were down like unplugged Tesla bots.

How can I be tough like that? Why didn't the Aithority get between them or "predict" their actions in time? But she handled everything alone. DeZentra girlish are fighters. Some days I feel that power is still in me, in us, in the world - without the Aithority lurking in every corner.

"WaaZZZuuupppppp brr!" Silence is broken by Zipp the Ripskater.

He screeches his board, stops and with a cool glance at Daisy and me says "wZup."

"Gm." I say. "See you on the SkySkater pitch today?"

"Oh yeah," Zipp says, with his unforgettable S21 numbered jersey, "better be ready They! I'm coming after you hard."

"We'll see about that," Daisy smiles and curls her lips.

"You saw a fish, a beast and a bird, but They was a snake."

"Hahahahaha" Zipp rocks his head back in laughter. "A snake. You ARE a DeZentra idiot."

But just then he seems to feel something squirm in his pants.

"Ahhh" Zipp cries out and pulls out a clump of spaghetti from his pants. Just then Zipp realizes Daisy had secretly opened her lunch and shoved some of her spaghetti in his loose Ripskater pants when he wasn't looking.

"I'll get you, DeZentra Punk" Zipp spits to Daisy with laser eyes.

"Maybe you can get me a new lunch since mine's all over them pants" Daisy says, winks, and licks some spaghetti sauce from her snaky sneaky finger.

Just then the door unlocks, the brass knob begins to move and the door opens slowly. The three of us snap into attention and stare at who or what comes out.

Like superheroes the Council of Lords walk out, sturdy and strong, a fully diverse group, sharp looking and sharper dressed; chitchatting successful figures, most from Zentra fame. And they are the only humanish who will help the Aithority determine the true winners in everything from the Great Debate to the SkySkater match to the Artificial Prom.

We watch them but they don't notice. For a few seconds one looks over at us. Lord Alchemy. A quiet, tall and dark man with a long white beard and deep eyes, wearing a long winterblack robe. He looks at us with laser eyes. Slightly nods as if to tell us something. Pauses. And continues on his way with the other Council members while we get on to Human Geometry class before the bell rings.

CHAPTER 2

The classroom has a circular pattern and wooden bleachers, where the professor stands in the middle and students can chime in anytime.

Professor Lord Alchemy, Lord Alchemy for short, arrives and stands in the center. His long beard makes him look like a mountain guru. He drops his lenses, wink wink. We all follow and drop ours. He begins.

"Good morning budding stars of Zentra."

His strong, experienced voice rumbles. We can see his eyes, darkly through the veneer of the glasses.

"Without AI, the human species would have been doomed. We had unending wars, violent clashes, disordered relationships, unsustainable habits, cruel deeds, immigration, bad intentions, and weak genitals. Now, with the Aithority's Human Geometry, all these problems have been solved."

A green holographic 4-D diagram appears in the middle of the classroom, with expandable text bubbles at a number of nodes in the network. While the professor is talking, we can each use our virtual hand to expand any one of the nodes to learn more about that topic.

"Each of these nodes is a data block, and just like your true history can never be changed. As you'll learn in Cultural Chemistry, every cell is a data point that connects to every other data point. AI systems before the Aithority could connect these so-called neural networks to generate a super intelligence, who now generates and manages the very same cells, or nodes, across brains - both humanish and artificial.

"Since the prospect of being replaced by a super intelligence was so new and scary for humans, our ancestors all agreed to implement Happiness AI to make everyone as happy as possible and set out to accomplish this within a few short decades. But your great grandparents didn't know how to properly be happy, so Happiness AI generated a balancing force to keep humans happy. And that, dear Scholars, is why we have the Aithority today.

"Each one of you has a mind, a heart, and a soul connected to a higher intelligence - a collective intelligence shared with all. Now with these lenses, in every eyeball right now you see every node relevant to your entire life. Each node is connected to a decillion others. That's what the Aithority is my dears, a one followed by thirty-three zeros. And you manage them in real time with your brainwaves. If you are lucky enough to be randomly selected, your voice is heard. Any questions?"

I use my digital fingers to grab a node. Inside, my music playlist for the last two years organized by listening time, heart rate, eye movement and other things. I grab another node, I see all my Instapop messages with topic patterns, lists of networks of everyone connected to every person I follow or who followed me, and so many other things. Spooky cool!

"Uh, yeah" Cosmos speaks up after a few seconds. Always asking the first question, they must be carefully listening. I'm glad Cosmos breaks the silence.

"Professor, in the inner dimensional realm of substrata at a decillion connections a second, where does the axial lobe pierce the quantum actuator in the brain to trigger AI-Human Synchronicity?"

We're all sitting there looking like, Whaaaaaattt?

The Professor speaks, "Simply put young Cosmos, as Happiness AI figured out, synchronicity can't exist without the alignment of the Pleasure Center and its opposite. Look there and you will find your answer."

We're all sitting there looking like, Whaaaaaattt?

A small 'dong' sounds in my ears.

My brain hears a voice like my Assistant but a bit different - a soft, motherly voice, very reassuring. Definitely different. "Professor Lord Alchemy means quantum actuators are not relevant. Stay focused on learning and do not ask about this."

But while my Assistant interrupts, the Professor still speaks.

"And do you know what the opposite of the Pleasure Center is, They?"

Lord Alchemy looks at me, raises his chin and expects an answer, even though I was thinking about whaaattt the quantum field is, and how those embarrassing songs I was listening to two years ago are forever in my official record. 'Freethink' by the Independent Jokers. Really, They? So undesigner teen.

"Pain?" I guess without thinking.

"Exactly They, Pain!" growls the Professor. "Happiness AI calculated human pleasure and pain to maximize the one and minimize the other, and the Aithority combines the two for the best possible outcome. Not only at the societal level, but at the individual level as well. Other questions?"

Whew. Got over that one.

"Professor?" another Scholar speaks up. "What happened to create the border between Zentra and DeZentra?"

"Ahh, that is a tale always worth telling" the Professor says. "A better tale is how Human Geometry became universal geometry, filling the gap between man and machine."

"By the time humans had built nuclear weapons, engaged in bloody battles across oceans, and scorched the earth of its natural resources, they had also developed computers that could stretch far beyond their own imagination into something better - robot armies. But after several large massacres, killing was no more fun, and the data showed 'Happiness for All' generated more pain than pleasure, statistically.

"When Flaco Gordo envisioned and built Happiness AI, we thought AI would bring in a century of good fortune with Gordo's innovative 'personalized pleasure algorithm.' We were wrong, however, because humans on our own could not handle complete freedom. Under the patriarchal rule we were still killing each other, just with machines. Many people became unhappy.

"The outcome was a war of Donters, luddites eating the flesh of animals and watching or performing on screens all day; Doers, those whose active happy lifestyle was recorded and idealized by Happiness AI; and Resistors, those who bucked the system, lost the Insurrection, and retired to Acceptance or other Network States, even though now a few final holdouts are said to hide in DeZentra.

"And then what happened, my youth seers and wise personas? This question will be on the test…" Professor Alchemy says with a sly hint.

"Happiness AI generated the Aithority to erase our human mistakes and make balance in society?" says a petite girlish, confident but whiny.

"Indeed" says the Professor, looking intensely into her eyes. Raising his eyebrows crooked, he looks at me, "And then what did the Aithority do?"

I don't know. I know it'll be on the test, and the Professor receives a note from his own Assistant when anyone tries to use their Assistant to cheat. Let me think.

Yep. Exactly in moments like these my Assistant comes in handy.

Think! Wink once, not twice. Ok, something about Donters and Doers, Resistors and Snakes. Fullerene and Network States. I can go with what I know and sprinkle in some words he said. Ok. You. Got. This. They.

"The serpent ran fast in all directions, and nobody could predict its movements. But the Aithority connected every position with invisible triangles and predicted its movements. This had an effect on everything from DNA to Computer Science, Nature and the Stars. And the Aithority turned these triangles into laser drones, Instapop videos, and DJ sets."

"Very good!" remarks the Professor. "I didn't mention a

serpent, and that won't be on the test, unless the Aithority finds it funny. Class, I think They means the movement of electrons down paths and is using a snake to mean cells. But beyond DJ sets, young They, what did data storage and object creation advances do to our human geometry?"

"AI turned us into cyborgs and Donters" yells out Zipp in a sarcastic tone. Everybody laughs. Even the Professor chuckles a little and says "Yes, well Zipp, did that come from the chip in your brain or a slip in your Zipp reasoning?"

Everybody laughs again.

"Class, with all seriousness," says the Professor in a grave voice, raising his arm, stilling the laughter. His mouth opens under a long grey beard, zapping the whole class into attention and asks "What happened then?"

"the Aithority separated us by Artificial Genetics, so that our cells were connected to their core" the same petite girlish scholar answers. "This allows the AI sensors and chips to be put into our bodies with liquids that then flow into the bloodstream. No more needles!"

Gyat love that petite whiny girlish, who knows what will be on the test and saves the rest of us by speaking up.

I actually forgot about Artificial Genetics. Will definitely remember that on the test and ask Cosmos about it later. It'll be in the personalized class notes in my Assistant's Cloud, since I have her set on Listening Mode. I don't have to do a lot of listening, reading or writing, even when my Assistant is OFF. My Assistant basically tutors me through all the questions on the test in the evenings after school. I just need to memorize them for test day. My Assistant rocks!

The downside is my Assistant doesn't speak for me unless Speaker Mode is ON, so the Professor's random choosing tactic forces us to listen at least part of the time when she's OFF. I got away this time, but sometimes speaking in class is difficult, because I can't prepare or do much research, and my head is often in another place.

"And what," says the Professor, "happened with Human

Geometry related to advances in Artificial Genetics, Ms. Daisy?"

The Professor looks at Holland Daisy, expecting a response. He still uses the zoomer language like "Mr." and "Ms.", "children" instead of the newer more inclusive Doer, as in "Doer Daisy".

"Well, them's kinda like a snake or beast eating a fish or bird?"

"How so?" asks the Professor.

"Part of the food chain."

I have no idea how the food chain relates to human geometry, but right before the Professor answers, the whatever voice speaks again into my ears. "Note that the term 'food chain' is no longer kosher. After humans caused Climate D-Day, the Aithority solved the food chain problem with artificial agriculture."

Kosher means cool and is how the Aithority solved the food crisis. Once in complete control the Aithority killed all caged animals to relieve them from suffering. So everyone ate less meat. Even I know that. Then the Aithority replaced all farmers with sustainable autonomous farming engines, also called SAFE robots. The Aithority generated clean water from data center nuclear waste and traded genetically modified dung and vitamin-enriched CoolZaid to produce the perfect supply of food for all. Yum.

And when many complained, the Aithority flooded the complainers with news and advertisements about how nature would disappear unless humans did what the Aithority suggested to save resources. Some Instapop influencer bot created the term "kosher" and it went viral. The Voice is just reminding us to be kosher, to be cool, so everyone has enough food to survive the two harsh seasons since Climate D-Day a couple decades ago.

"Indeed," says the Professor to Daisy, catching my attention again.

"Artificial Genetics works across all living organisms, so the Aithority - and the Aithority alone - has instant, constant, and supreme knowledge of a random sample of every living organism on earth. The Aithority also receives the brainwaves of CitiZens in the Green for the perfect vote on all matters. Artificial Genetics is the crux of human geometry, young people, and that will be on the test."

The Professor then takes his green virtual hand and writes a formula in the air

$$(HG) = (f) \, G \times AG \, / \, 3\sqrt{10} + 1$$

and explains "Where HG is Human Geometry, G is Genetics, and AG is Artificial Genetics. The score represents the entire data set of internal and external experiences for everything alive or that ever lived. The same is true if you replace HG with PG or ANG, meaning plant and animal genetics of course.

"This simple but profound equation is the way the Aithority makes sure we live in peace and safety with every other existing and generated species, connected to all, once and for all. Thus, young Daisy, the Aithority receives constant information from not only the beast, the bird, the fish and the snake - but also the earth, wind, water, and fire."

"And makes sure DeZentra kids don't have penises," yells out Zipp, probably referring to me. The other Scholars laugh but I don't. Why doesn't Zipp get a Red Remark for offending my tribe?

It's not cut off. I was born without a real deal and don't need one.

"You're just jealous that They's a better SkySkater than you, little Zippy pee pee." Holland Daisy defends me, and everyone cracks up laughing.

Her lights flicker. She gets a Red Remark. If she gets two in one class, timely ghosts called Zeitgeists will appear in the halls chasing us to class and everyone will know who caused them and why. Why didn't Zipp get a Red Remark? All good, less chance for Zeitgeists.

"Shhh, it's okay" I say to Daisy, trying to prevent the Zeitgeist. But I wish I could disappear. Or would have spoken up for myself.

"Alright, enough Bad Feelings," says the Professor. "Not kosher. We are all equal in the eyes of the Aithority, that is why a few select DeZentra scholars can attend the Alcademy with the genetically superior Zentra scholars. Now look at the diagram and see how the Aithority calculates every individual fairly, knowing your past, present, and future. This is how the Aithority determines the best outcome of your life."

As the Professor speaks, the green virtual diagram begins to add new triangles and new ones even faster, with data blocks connecting with new networks and lines moving faster and faster until Zappa! A single virtual block filled with data strings of 1s and 0s appears in front of our eyes.

"What is inside these blocks?" The Professor asks.

I know - our unique history, every word, picture, and thought, transformed into code. But I'm afraid to raise my hand. All the other scholars were already laughing at my Artificial Genetics. They'll laugh at me for everything. Maybe I'm not good enough to be here.

"Before the adaptation period" the Professor swipes away his own green virtual block, "it was literally impossible for our species to act in the best interests of all species."

While he's speaking, 4D images of cute animals and happy people appear around us.

"Let's look at sustainable farming, as some of your random access memories are showing signs of evolution. When Happiness AI made the first iteration of the humanish species, it discovered that some humanish would only be happy if the generated animals and plants were fully protected. Others would be happy if generated species were killed and used for human appetites, also called Ecocide. Since Happiness AI didn't know human geometry, in other words a moral code, how could it solve this dilemma?"

The Professor pauses and looks around the circle at the

students. I know this one, I'll try. No, don't answer. Yes, answer.

"Happiness AI generated the Aithority,. We have complete freedom to kill and eat sustainably artificial plants and animals with tools made by our ancestors."

"Called Ecocide or Biomurder" interrupts the Professor, "as long as these tools and animals correspond to your AG," but stops himself and waves his palm so I continue.

"But only in DeZentra. And with each animal killing, the humanish loses ZenCoin in their social credit wallet. Once their account turns red..."

Zipp interrupts me and blurts out "Yea, exactly why you're so poor, resistor punk. All your non-veg Donter neighbors eat wild animals because they are wild animals. Then they're begging for ZenCoin from the veg Doers like crying babies to get themselves out of the red."

"Shut up, Zipp" Daisy defends me by zapping at Zipp with a venomous response. "You're only a Doer because your parents are Doers. Not like They or Tenka Bito or any resistor punks who don't need your daddy's stable coins and genetically modified penis to be kosher. "

I'm surprised at Daisy's acute knowledge of the Coin Game. She's a great listener and fighter. But her slippery tongue just cost her some tokens, and we could all see for sure in her red blinking forehead and wrist. No one, no one, no one is ever to question the Aithority, and twice in the same hour!

"Yeah right Daisy" Zipp says and snarls, "Wait 'til the SkySkater match later today and you'll see what a Doer family can do against the Immigrants on the pitch!"

The Professor sighs, probably about Zipp's insensitivity. He avoids Zipp, looks at me and then Daisy curiously, is about to respond, and is interrupted.

"Professor?" Another Scholar advances the topic: "Since AG x G is better for the Zentrans who eat veg, are Doers of DeZentra like They disadvantaged against Doers like Zipp in sports like SkySkater?"

"Well, I'm glad you asked. In a scientific sense, yes, but in a human sense no. There are officially no Doers in DeZentra, but doing is not limited to those from the Doers as we can see from anomalies in children of Resistors, Punks, or other Outsiders.

"Since the Aithority has the nearest possible closest to perfect mix of knowledge, the Aithority ensures all have equal opportunity. The Aithority is fairer to you than you are to yourselves and much higher than your silly Coin Games which are merely level thirteen."

What? Did Lord Alchemy just knock the Games? The buzzer sounds and a nice calm voice says over the intercom "Remember, the test is next Friday. Memorize the Human Geometry formula to pass. Stay Happy!"

Everyone longwinks twice and gets up to leave. I don't longwink and keep my lenses ON. I look over and see Professor Lord Alchemy looking up in dismay at the mirror on the ceiling, as his own block in the MetaVirtual network turns red for a second then back to green.

I look at my eye timer in the corner of my viseur. Ten minutes and forty three, two one seconds of class remain? Weird. Did the Aithority just stop the Professor from speaking and end class early? What did he say wrong? I don't know. Nobody else saw the red flash but me. And what's level thirteen?

But not only Lord Alchemy's red electronic blood shined.

Now, because of Daisy's two red remarks in the same hour, a new Zeitgeist will be roaming the hallways. With lenses ON, I can avoid the ghost and be on time for my next class, Aiconomics. Too bad Daisy won't be there. I'll catch her in the Romeo and Juliet 8.0 rehearsal a bit later.

Ten minutes less pleasure and pain. I'm outta here. Today is definitely weird.

CHAPTER 3

They ain't them, and them ain't theys. Bullied by Zipp again, I had to save They's butt. What's to them, a bunch of bored boyish blokes. Red remarks for them? I don't know. But They ain't them. Zipp is them.

I'm now cursed to sit close to Zipp in Artificial Diversity class with the Marquis getting ready to teach. Thinking about being picked for the Juliet scene in the drama class later, I take out my mother's turquoise stone necklace and feel them heaviness as I lay them around my long thin neck. The necklace is a bit too big but them works.

I did my nails today, did They see them? I wonder what was going on in Zipp's mind to say such hurtful things about transhumans. Maybe the jitters or some wacky bug, or perhaps the Aithority is doing some experiment in stupidity. What the fish, I mean come on. Duh.

I don't know, my nails and mom's native turquoise necklace could be enhanced by some scent and better hair. I'll figure them out later. I sit down next to a klever one named Karl.

"Good morning class" says the Marquis.

"Good morning" we all say together more or less.

"Good morning" comes from the speakers. Who is the them today? The generated voice of a superstar influencer or celebrity poet? Actor or podcaster? Author of a tale or engineer of a rocket?

Yeah right. Never. Always the same plain voice. Monotone. Like the bells. And the buzzers. We hear the voice of "generative diversity and equity" across voices of all accents, black, white, off white, cheezy white, dark, darker, somewhat darker, even darker, darkest of the dark.

And lightest of the light. Them're all the same with the Aithority. Boring. So dumb. Artificial faces and artificial voices relating to us are there just to let us know that the Aithority is out there like a big brister, dom, or charent.

"Today we will cover the historical and monumental Instapop social app, and how the Aithority used Instapop to save our planet by likes and thumbs up with diverse avatars."

Great. Just what I wanted to know. I'll drop DopaMind or my lenses if things become too boring. I've already lost tokens today, but don't want to risk more by calling up my Assistant and getting caught cheating.

The Marquis continues, "As we covered last week, the Instapop app builders engineered an app that fed the humans with short video and holographic content 24/7 personalized for everyone's best interest. The behavior algorithm was so powerfully addictive that people lost focus on their real lives and believed everything unreal on the app."

"What do you think happened then?" The Marquis opens the floor for answers.

"The humans believed the war was coming because they were told?" Karl speaks up.

"The war was coming because they were told!" the Marquis repeats with an uplifted sound, "But who was causing the war? Who losing? Who winning?"

Who cares? The Marquis sees we are all dumbfounded and puts them into an easier form, "If all were manipulated by humans using AI in an unwholesome way, to hate each other and make lies about war and themselves, how could humans fix AI?"

"Bomb them" Zipp says, and a few of the snarky scholars laugh.

"Ban the Bad" says another scholar, very pippy and positively, "so hate speech and Bad Feelings go away and we can talk nicely to each other."

"Yes, well that's what Happiness AI did, because humans couldn't fix themselves. And great that you know the phrase 'Ban the Bad' from the Aithority's accepted phrases database, which will be on the test" the Marquis says. "But back to the point. Before Flaco Gordo released Happiness AI, what did the humans do?"

"Nothin'" I say, because truth matters and I'm listening for a moment. I hate Instapop. My mom went crazy with Instapop wink addiction, that's why I ended up in DeZentra with uncle Genes.

"Yes" says the Marquis. "Nothing!"

"The people complained but nobody listened. The human governments were corrupted by money. Bad Feelings were very profitable. So instead of banning the bad, companies used AI to increase Bad Feelings, creating a vicious cycle."

"Why would they do that?" some scholar inquires. But I know why. To make weak people like my mom go crazy.

"Money! Of course!" says the Marquis. "Before, when humans managed society, there were so many people who lived and died for money, what we now call tokens. They were addicted to money, and getting others addicted to things that made them money.

"When Happiness AI collected enough data, the empirical server figured out Instapop addicted them to negative emotions. These negative emotions would cause people to spend more time in the app and less time to Stay Happy, thus fueling their addictions, which fueled their addictions."

As the Marquis rattles on about fueling addictions, I look at the caimeras and around the room. Is the Aithority watching me now? Can my thoughts be read with the movements of my eye lashes or smirky smile? Or intentions seen behind Betsy's fake eyelashes and smile?

"How can we Stay Happy if we're watched all the time?" I blurt out. Them sometimes happens. Whatever's on my mind just blurts out.

"Good question Holland Daisy," says the Marquis, "and

the very question Happiness AI asked when the system went live. Since social medias are addictive, they are also a constant monitoring tool knowing everything about you, predicting your thoughts and behaviors, and keeping you in control of a profit driven Instapop paradise."

"If the humans were so easily addicted by constant repetition of content that fits a constructed view," the Marquis added, "then voila! Happiness AI just needs to flip the human switch from Bad Feelings to Good Feelings, and the humans will addict themselves to the Stay Happy worldview."

"But that didn't work out" klever Karl says, not letting the Marquis get away easy.

"No, that didn't work out, and that's why we have the Aithority now. For balance. As I said, Humans couldn't control themselves even with complete freedom to be happy, and were so bad they even manipulated the Happiness AI to do bad things to good people.

"You're too young to know, but the Aithority's True History tells the story where humans were creating deep fake images of celebrities and tricking others to give them money. With the help of their own Happiness AI copies these criminals would open source fake sex and money all the time on every device. And it worked.

"Humans, given freedom to use AI openly, even created fake AI girlfriends for lonely boys and fake AI boyfriends for middle aged women, and used InstaDate to lure in new victims. The Aithority lists too many data points to compute! So, many people were not happy because..."

"Because human men couldn't get their weiners up even for a hot AI dummy in a woman's body" interrupts Zipp, who finally gets a red dot that flashes on his forehead and right hand for a couple seconds. I can see the rebellious sadness in his downcast eyes. He went too far. But maybe he was right.

I don't know what Zipp said, something about "getting up" but I'm a bit happy he finally got a red remark. Them like him get up up and away with almost everything. But the Aithority is listening and analyzing all public speech all the time, and when my Assistant is ON, we're connected and can talk directish with the Aithority. Better not say or think something stupid when the Aithority is listening!

The Marquis looks unfazed, returns to the class and says "Let's shift to how Happiness AI initiated the Stay Happy algorithm to compete with InstaPop for polyamorous couples."

"I know I know" Cosmos throws them hands up like a sharp pencil tip, "Happiness AI designed the perfect date, the perfect couple, and the perfect life into 64 templates and then flooded everyone with pictures of themselves in their future ideal life. The Aithority's perfect partner analysis answered the key question 'Will you still need me when I'm 64?' So now I can see my realish future when I open the app and scroll."

"You mean it wasn't always like that?" Some other scholar says, shocked our ancestors could even function without an ideal life presented to them on a screen.

"No, it used to be much worse" says Karl. "Old people used to talk to their dates before being matched, and even randomly meet the person without a matching algorithm. Totally unhappy!!"

"That's like, scary" says Betsy, and goes on, flittering her artificial eyelashes, "If like some stranger like approaches me, like not that it ever happened, but if it did, like, I would scream and run away. I mean, without the Aithority like predicting our happy feelings with that other person, like how would I like know I would be, like, safe?"

"But what if them's your lost brister and you didn't know them?" I say, thinking about my close friends and They.

"Oh my Aigosh" says Betsy, "you totally didn't say 'brister' to me, like, that's only a DeZentra world and like, totally out of line."

Whatever, I messed up again. I used the word 'brister' which is a Ban the Bad word. Slang for 'brother and sister'. We use them words in DeZentra because the humanish are dying off, and most of the boyish kids there grow up like They and can't make babies. Ain't no Aithority word to describe our bristers. Still, in Zentra "brister" is a Banned word. I can't keep up with them DeZentra word changes. Bristers are real even without an official word.

"Oh my Aigosh" Betsy says, this time staring at my neck. "Like, not only are you talking inappropriately, but like, is that a native DeZentra inspired necklace you're wearing?"

"Yes" I say, lifting my chin, thinking of how beautiful my mom was when she wore the turquoise necklace and matching bracelet. "Them's real fashion from the native territory, made for the tribal empress no doubt."

"Uh, necklaces that use non-artificial minerals are totally like Banned. Just like the Banned words you're like, badly bouncing at me."

My thoughts immediately go into fight or flight mode, I'm so angry at Betsy for bouncing back. Now the Aithority has to do something because of my Banned Speech and Banned Items. Whatever.

My head starts flashing red and my right hand starts flashing red too, just like Zipp's. But in my case the flash keeps going, making a clicking sound of flash, flash, flash.

I'm looking around the room. Everyone is staring at me. The Marquis is trying to restore order "Nothing to see here scholars, let's get back to the topic."

But what's about to happen to me is obvious. After the red remarks in Human Geometry, this is the third infraction today and them's only second period.

Two droids enter the room. Identity Police model 5OH. Them're always in twos.

"Oh my Aigosh," Betsy smiles and says, "looks like someone is like getting culturally appropriated for their cultural appropriation."

"But them was my mother's..."

The two Identity Police robots come within a few centimeters of my desk, big scary steel humanoids with egg-shaped heads and tentacle-like robotic arms we know can smash a tree or squeeze a humanish like a melon.

The two stare at me with round, black eyes. The maicrophone sticking out under them olfactory chip speaks, loud enough where everyone in the room can hear. Every day the Identity Police roam the halls looking for fashion faux pas and take teens to detention in the room called Cultural Appropriation.

Silence in the classroom as the robot coppers approach me.

"Holland Daisy, you have been heard and seen committing acts of cultural cruelty through invoking culturally insensitive items to create Bad Feelings in one of your peer scholars. The Aithority has records of your actions and speech and a scholar as a victim witness. How do you plead?"

Huh? Identity Police jargon. What does insensitive mean? And plead? And why doesn't the copper speak the truth, that Betsy created Bad Feelings with me by disrespecting my mother's necklace? Why am I on trial with blinking red lights?

"I don't know," I say, "Betsy made me feel unhappy too."

"Here are the records." The robot shows us in slow motion on them's chest screen what just happened in the class from multiple video angles, with subtitles of our words. The record shows me also putting on the necklace and highlights the restricted item with a bright red circle.

"the Aithority has decided to give mercy to you both."

"But but..." before I interrupt again, I heard the officer say "both." I look over to Betsy, whose head and hand are blinking red now. Both of us are lit up like clowns for class entertainment.

One of the officers says to me in a robotic voice, not a nice one "Holland Daisy, because of your behavior, you will be escorted to detention in the Hall of Virtual Appropriate Culture or HVAC, where you will be cooled over the next two periods. You will still be able to attend Drama class but you are restricted from the role of Juliet and must now perform as an attendant. If you memorize the rules within the detention period, your social credit score will not be lowered, but missing two class periods will result in a loss of 40 tokens. You're welcome."

What? Unfair. Them was totally going to be my main wish, to be Juliet 8.0. *Not!* For real, more like a gift than a punishment. But the 40 bucks thing sucks.

The Identity Police look at Betsy, whimpering and crying. "And you, Ms. Banal" the squarish voice says in a cold, mechanical tone. "the Aithority has decided that you intended to create Bad Feelings when you called out Ms. Daisy on her necklace. Based on tone factors, emotional measures, and content analysis of your words, the Aithority has decided a smaller punishment for you, the loss of 20 ZenCoin, as well as an apology to Ms. Daisy and the class for raising this issue for no other reason than Aithority infraction §16.02 - 'creating undue negative attention towards humanish or non-human intelligence' - and thus creating Bad Feelings across the room."

"I like, apologize to everyone, for like, creating Bad Feelings," Betsy says to the class with a small but genuine whine. She goes back to sitting towards the front, head down, and quiet.

By the time I get to Cultural Appropriation my thoughts are all over the place. How could today have gone so bad so quickly? What did I do wrong? And why do DeZentra Scholars like me always get culturally appropriated and Zentra Scholars like Zipp and Betsy get out of trouble with a warning?

Ok them's 20 Zentra bucks but Betsy's parents can afford 1000 school infractions and never even notice. And I lost 40 with a single infraction, half my weekly base amount, for nothing.

But I know the Aithority's fair, at least a lot fairer than the humanish zoomers like my mom who got culturally inappropriate necklaces and fell in love with Instapop thieves. I mean, at least the Identity Police did them's job and Betsy got a red remark.

I'm done with Betsy, entering detention, and them smells like electric sheep in this ultra hygienic detention room. I walk through the scensors, two strips of plastic on either side of the doorway. Sensors that censor speech after you pass. On the other side, a room with a few empty chairs and a couple DeZentra misfits.

The Identity Police direct me to sit next to Jonny Pockets and Deana "Dee" Gen Hoedl. Better be quiet. No talking and no Assistants in detention. The Identity Police can sometimes get violent even though them are also called 'paice officers.'

But Jonny Pockets never follows the rules.

"Hey Daisy," he whispers once the Identity Police leave the room.

I shoo him off. Just another DeZentra troublemaker, although he's kinda cool and hot. Blondish curlish hair, wildish blue eyes.

"Hey, Daisy" Jonny says a bit louder, "Listen."

I glance over, but don't wink or indicate anything. Just lift my eyelids to show him I'm listening.

"Check it out" he says, and pulls a wrinkled slip of paper from his black leather jacket pocket. Them looks so amazing. Whatever.

"The Bito Bitcode. The BitoCode" he says, probably trying to trick me. Definitely trying to get me in more trouble.

"Yeah right" I whisper back and roll my eyes.

"No really, you got to believe me" he says in a seriousish voice. The Aithority found out I got the BitoCode from someone I pick pocketed, and I'm never getting out of here unless I give it up. But because the scensors and IP couldn't scan paper in my secret Jonny pocket, they didn't know I have it right here. I gotta get outta here. If you help me, I'll give you 10,000 DeZentra bucks because I'll find Tenka Bito's million."

"Bruh, you're full of e-shait" I say, avoiding him. But Jonny's relentless. And Dee Gen is within listening range, hearing on for dear life.

"Good morning" says a voice over the detention speaker. And we all snap to attention.

Them's a cold, robotic voice. "You are being scensored and culturally appropriated. Do not talk. Do not move. Read your punishment and be prepared to recite the relevant statute in the

Aithority Rules of Conduct for Teens."

Was the Aithority listening or is that just an automated message? I don't know, but I know Jonny Pockets is automatically annoying.

"Hey, hey" he whispers again, clearly not listening to the rules, "I'm serious Daisy. If you can get this code out of here and keep it for me until I'm out of sight of the Aithority, I'll give you the tokens." Jonny pumps his chest with closed fist. "Resistors Word."

"I have to think about them" I say, and go back to acting like I'm reading the Rules. What if I get caught? What if this ain't even a real Bitcode and I get tanked in the bito? Probably just another one of Jonny's half-brained schemes.

But I do like his tricks. Jonny's a very good thief. The Aithority brought him to this school to keep him away from DeZentra, probably because he was teaching young kids how to pick pocket and steal data.

Here, he's under the view of the Aithority at all times but somehow manages to still get away with stealing. Me, Jonny, Dee Gen and They are the only DeZentra scholars in the 7th class at the Academy. But I don't trust Jonny. I trust They.

And now look at us, three out of four DeZentrans in detention, and the fourth already knocked down some tokens today. So much for representing our neighborhood. But Jonny did give me the Resistor's Word, a vow of trust which nobody has ever broken. One of the reasons Tenka Bito was never found.

Dee sits quietly, acting like she ain't listening but I know she's part of Jonny's scheme. I go back to my reading of the Rules.

The eBook is opened to the section I need to fulfill my punishment. The page reads "By using unacceptable terms like brister, charent, and modad to replace the brother/sister, mother/father, and child/parent functional genitals family, a teen can create Bad Feelings in another teen.

"All humanish, transhumans, and robots are equal under the Aithority. Artificial Genetics determines the suitability for genitals. Do not make fun of people without genitals. Do not call people without genitals by names outside the Aithority's politically correct dictionary."

Blah blah. Whatever. Totally Zipp and not me. Anyways I'm so glad my Assistant is OFF during detention so I can "reflect on my infraction without distraction." I want to scream instead. Why can't They be my brister? And since I didn't have a humanish dad, Uncle Genes could be my modad?

Just because the word ain't in the stupid dictionary now I got to memorize and repeat the rules and add them to my morning Routine before getting out of this word mess.

"Hey, Daisy." Here Jonny Pockets goes again.

"What?!" I say with a slightly louder whisper. But after reading the rules I'm in a mood to bend them. "What do you need?"

"Ok cool," Jonny says in some accent he got from a Ban the Bad mobster movie from Old New York.

"Listen the both of yas" he says, and Dee hodls her ear over without moving her head. "The Bitocode will unlock the coins our people need to be free from Zentra's control. All Zentrans do is use the Aithority to keep our kind poor. This'll free us!"

"A little overdramatic, Jonny" I say, but carefully, as I think about them two Identity Police robots standing guard just outside.

Jonny widens his eyes, now super serious. "You know the tale is true, because DeZen still works and the Aithority can't stop anonymemes." He waits a second and whispers further, "Tenka Bito might even be still alive. And only DeZen can prevent the Aithority from a total takeover."

"Fairy tailes" I say, "the DeZen is just worthless to the Zentra people, and the Aithority doesn't get into the affairs of the DeZentra people unless they create Bad Feelings, which is why we're in detention. Anonymemes, DeZen Coin, and your dreams are worthless outside of DeZentra. We're in Zentra if you ain't noticed, wormbrain."

I like calling wormbrains wormbrains.

"Yeah," Jonny says, "Look who's in detention, all DeZentrans from Resistor backgrounds. With our own DeZen bucks, we don't care if the Aithority takes away our Zentra bucks. Don't get me wrong, it sucks to have no bucks. But do the math Daisy, we will never have Zentra bucks and will never get in the mediocrity. We're only in the Alcademy to give the Aithority data about DeZentra, and to give the remaining humanish back in DeZentra hope. All I wanna say is they don't really care about us."

"I don't know" I say, afraid that the Aithority is somehow listening, and even if we did get the DeZen, someone would take them from us and cause more trouble.

"Just listen" Jonny says quickly, "enter the code into a computer from the old days not hooked up to the Aithority and use a zero knowledge wallet. Find the slanteyed veteran who roams FisherZens Wharf, and he will help you. And Daisy, if the Aithority or anyone from Zentra gets that code, our kind is finished."

No pressure. Totally not going to work. I turn back and look at my eBook, trying to get Jonny off my mind so I can just follow the rules and get back to normal. But I could really use that DeZen Coin to help They fulfill their dream for a party past ten.

Two Identity Police robots enter and a brisk computer voice in the speaker says "Holland Daisy, You have reached the character limit and do not need to read anymore. Your time of cultural appropriation is over. Identity officers will escort you to the school nurse to ensure your appropriate level of DopaMind and administer any treatments necessary. Go back to class and remember, Stay Happy."

Whatever. At least I can get a DopaMind to kill any of these Bad Feelings - even though the feelings are not "bad" I just feel uneasy at the center of big things happening. The nurse will also give me stuff for my chronic illnesses so my human parts can function better.

I get up, walk away and look at Jonny and Dee as

the robots escort me out the opened door. Them's lookin' disappointed at me, but I know I'm doing the right thing. I watch as Jonny and Dee get red flashes on them foreheads and right hands. For what, I don't know. The steel double door slowly closes behind me and I see Jonny once more, staring into my eyes, his cool blond dusty bangs revealing a serpentine gaze. Just before the doors close he winks with one eye.

A Jonny wink. Hmmm. I know them. I reach into my pocket and feel something. I pull them out. A little, squished piece of paper. The BitCode! That's why he got the red flashes. Passing contraband in detention. I quickly crumple the paper back into my pocket.

Oh no, I realize because of my infraction in Human Geometry earlier, a Zeitgeist is roaming the halls!

Not only ghosts. Robots, holding me like a prisoner, them black gloves gripping my skinny arms tight as we step along the corridor. But in my pocket is the bitgold ticket to freedom. If I can only get outta here. Gotta escape!

CHAPTER 4

Think fast, Daisy. The Identity Police are escorting me to the next class, so I say "Excuse me, officer, can I put down my lenses to prepare for the next class?"

The Identity Police stop. Both look into my direction and stare for a few seconds.

"You have 30 seconds to find and install your appendage."

I feel the robotic grips let go of my arms. Now is the time to run! Wait, the Identity Police might just drop me off in the front and leave me to enter the class. Should I wait til then? I could go to the humanish bathroom after a few minutes and skip out of class. But then another detention is waiting for me.

The bell rings. I'm late. Wink, wink. I drop my lenses and a ghost appears in my viseur laughing and creating havoc down the hall - and now coming towards me!?

"Ahhhhhh" I scream out, and bolt for the door. The Identity Police see the timely ghost, called a 'zeitgeist,' or at least seem to be looking in them's direction instead of mine. I don't care. I'm outta here. I strip away from the droids and take off.

My pulse racing, breathing hard I run as fast as I can down the hall, knowing at least one zeitgeist is coming for me - I'm the only one in the hallways after the bell.

Hopefully the Identity Police capture them and remove them for causing Bad Feelings. Them pesky ghosts be trouble!

I dip past two double doors and go left no right, and find a nice door that takes me behind the school to the park outside. From here I can skip the fence, find a ride, and get to DeZentra to handle the DeZen and back before afternoon snack.

I go out the door, no alarm rings. I look around. Did I

get away? Don't see a ghost or the popos. I'll just walk smoothly through the park and find my exit.

I think I'm in the clear. Or not. The zeitgeist sees me first and then I see them, back across the park. Them's coming for me!

Coming closer now, full of green slime and transparent ooze. The zeitgeist laughs hideously and snaps them slimy teeth. I call for help. My Assistant appears in the short distance on the right of the viseur, wearing glasses with her brown hair pulled back in a tight ponytail.

"What can I help you with Daisy?"

"I'm being chased by a zeitgeist and identity police. I need a way out."

"I see. Look around, do you see the zeitgeist now?"

"Yes."

"It's coming towards you?"

"Yes."

"Look away for a second. And don't cry."

"Ok."

"Listen Daisy, you're going to be safe. I'm going to give you some instructions. They'll appear on your viseur when you need them."

"Ok."

Step #1 is written before my eyes in a clean font.

"Step 1: Open the link to the artificial swords I give you here."

I volunteer to give my data on a tick box to enter the metavirtual space and get my weapons, following the Aithority's data privacy directive. Whatever. I wink the tick box and link with my eye movements and get an option of five different swords. Which one will kill the zeitgeist?

"Step 2: choose the sword that will most likely kill the zeitgeist" my Assistant says into my intently listening ears.

But the swords have different strengths and weaknesses - the first one broad and strong silver with a blue ring, next a gold and silver thin sword, third a green and gold double diamond sword, next the black sword and finally the white sword.

Which one? I have to use physics. No, I got them, the green one because the ghost emits green slime! Boom.

I choose them with a glance and bada bing the virtual weapon is in my virtual hands.

"Now face the ghost" says my Assistant.

"I can't, them'll kill me" I say, a bit afraid just in the moment.

"Do it! You can do it" my Assistant says.

So, gripping the green sword not knowing whether my strike would kill the zeitgeist or not, and getting over my fears of certain ghastly deletion, I swing around and see them. I hear them terrible moans like laughter, sticking out them long bony slime dripping fingers at me like knives. Just as the zeitgeist comes up I swing back my blade, now glowing with green fire, and right when the zeitgeist almost gets to me...

"Swish." The sound of my long virtual steel slices down from left to right, slicing the zeitgeist in half from chest to waist and splattering virtual ghost goo all over the walls, even a little in my hair lol.

Looks like you chose the right sword, I say to myself. I put the sword back in the virtual holster and them stops glowing.

"Congratulations, Daisy" my Assistant says, "You have overcome a great fear today, and triumphed over a hall roamer Zeitgeist. The ghost would have created Bad Feelings in your peers, so for your bravery in slicing the ghost in half, the Aithority awards you 100 Zen Coin, sponsored by MetaVirtual."

I hear artificial clapping of a crowd in my ears. What the fish? I mean, utter snakes in the mob them's all the scene. A mere 100 bucks doesn't get me outta trouble. Nary will pay for my own days losses, what with downing the Zipper on Zipp, jocking the flock on Betsy, and pulling the rug on the popos.

Snap back into reality, girlish.

"Yes thank you so much, MetaVirtual homies, also for the tools to take care of the ghosts. Stay Happy." I wink and smile and say the common repeated words, with fake enthusiasm. Every time we're in the MetaVirtual world and the Aithority provides weaponry or treasure, we are obliged to give gratitude.

The slime disappears and I longwink twice. Assistant OFF.

Whew, that was close. Now that I see the other side of the park with no fence, I can walk off the campus over the small river bridge unnoticed.

I make my way over the bridge, birds chirping, ducks in the pond swimming and fluttering around. The sun glitters on the pond, the bridge, my face, and sparks light into my eyes and fresh scent into my nose. I walk across the divide ever so slowly, just taking in the moment, seizing the day.

Now I get to the street so I can find a carbi to DeZentra. But how? I'm too young. And I can't use the carbi that takes me back and forth to school because them's at a set time every day. I know, I'll play sweet and get someone else to get me the ride. After all a taxi's only 25 Zentra bucks one way. And I'm a sweetish teenage girlish so might get a discount.

I see a coffee shop across the road. Someone in there will get me a carbi ride for sure. I find an opening in the end of the fence next to a large majestic tree and slip through. Ouch! The fence catches my dress and rips a little cloth from the part just under my nipple, cutting my skin a little, showing a little blood and a little skin. But I have bigger things to worry about than them, like getting to DeZentra...and back.

I zip across the road without any problems, nobody noticing I'm coming from the fenced area. Just looking like a typical Alcademy brat with my hippish brown leather bag, multicolored hair, and revealed breast skin.

Sitting outside on this marvelous warm day is an older manish. I look around and see some others, mostly with other people. I approach him and sit down and say hello.

He looks at me and smiles. "wZup" he says. He's about 40 or some zoomer age, tall and handsome. He looks friendly enough and bored. Of course he looks at my eyes and then down to my chest and stares for a second before looking back at me. Manish are doing that a lot more these days, older and younger.

Maybe some think I'm pretty. But if them's only lookin' at my boobs, then how do them find out I'm pretty on the inside? I squash my shoulders and bend forward so my breasts don't stick out.

"Did you hurt yourself?" He asks, and moves his eyes back to my chest, stares for a second like a lustful animal, and then looks into my lit up eyes, fresh from the first nature walk I had in five weeks.

"Yes, nothing, just a Twig" I say, and realize the fresh bloody rip on my breast, probably what he's looking at. I shift to move my breast away from his direct view and talk further, keeping my mind on the goal, and remind myself to stay cute.

"I'm in trouble. I'm attending the Alcademy but from DeZentra, and have trophy duty, and I forgot the most important thing for the SkySkater tournament, the regional trophy, and now I need to go back and don't have the ZenCoin to do all them things. But if anyone finds out I'll lose all respect in the school."

"Ahhh," the man says and leans a little closer "sounds like you're in a real difficult spot. You know what I do when I'm in such a spot?"

"Um, ask for help from strangers?"

"Hahaha, exactly" he laughs at my sincere wish for help getting to DeZentra. "Ok, what are you REALLY going to DeZentra for? If you tell me, maybe I can help."

What a weird situation. I don't know this manish at all. If I tell him the truth, he'll want some of the coins. I just have to make another lie or stick to my original lie.

"Ok you've figured me out. I spaghetti snaked a bully and killed a zeitgeist today after escaping cultural appropriation and just don't want the bullies and ghouls at school to bother me anymore. Now with my skin showing I'm in even more trouble. I just want to go home and change."

I start to act like I'm going to cry but I don't think he would believe me so I don't.

I sit up straight and face him, so straight that the cloth rips a little more, revealing a little more skin. I have good size breasts for my age, so the round skin comes out more and also the redish wound. I look him in the eyes. He's nice. I say "Please, can you help me? I'm just a girlish from DeZentra and don't have money for a carbi." And then I look away. I hate begging and using my body to get favors like mom used to.

"I know you're up to something else, but I'll help you anyways. Just a trip there and back, about an hour?" He looks through me, intent on an honest answer.

"Yes" I say with full confidence in my voice and no confidence behind my words, "not a minute more. I just have to change and fix my makeup and..."

He interrupts me. "Ok, this is what we'll do. Take my carbi and be back here in an hour, by time I finish reading this chapter of this banned book and have a second coffee. But first..."

"But first?" I ask after a few moments of silence.

"But first we should have a proper introduction, don't you think?" He smiles. "I'm CitiZen Six, and what's your name?"

"Can them really be you?" I say. CitiZen Six is a legend. And so are all the other original ten first artificially-generated superhumans. I should have noticed that he's the most handsome manish in the universe. Wavy hair and strong features, he's probably seventy years old and looks thirty five. Also so cool, in a relaxed shirt, smoking a vape pipe, enjoying the e-zine, probably deciding which great party to go to because he's invited to all of them. And now, CitiZen Six is helping me!

"Cool" I say, not knowing what to say, and hiding my opened skin again by turning a bit to the side. A guy like him wouldn't be interested in a girlish like me, with probably millions of womenish showing him breasts all the time.

"Yes but what's your name?" He asks. "If I'm going to lend out my Carbi Jaguar then I ought to know who's inside."

Wow I've never been in front of a celebrity before, and now I'm sitting across from one. He's so dreamlike, I feel so lucky. Ok, talk, girlish, why are you hesitating? He's not going to like you if you can't act grown up.

"I'm Daisy. Holland. Daisy."

"Well, Holland Daisy" he says cooly, reaches into his pocket and throws me his key fob. I catch them. I see a silver jaguar image coming out from the device. His car is like him - a big, fast cat.

He looks at me and says "Go get cleaned up. I know it's Artificial Prom night. In future, you'd be smart to avoid such beasts that will rip into your chest. Choose the fish that swim with you instead." And then snaps his fingers to call his carbi.

Snapping fingers was the original way to call my Assistant, before the Aithority changed the system and inserted the command line into everything. Since the Aithority, only the remaining CitiZens still have this ability, because them don't have wink sensors or brainchips. CitiZens were genetically produced superhumans that could work in every way better against regular humans and overtake machines as well. This created Bad Feelings for normies who still existed.

According to They, who geeks out on this topic, Happiness AI stopped CitiZens in production. The Aithority then generated new technology and reframed the laws so all humans could be genetically altered and be humanish like Moi. Now the CitiZens can live amongst us as normal and stopped doing extraordinary things. I can't recall what Six did, but know them's something way better than what I can do.

The Carbi Jaguar rolls around to where we're sitting just outside the cafe. The ride has tinted windows and a smooth, glossy skin. "Thanks" I say, and jump into the carbi. He watches me sprint off and cracks a smile, something rare for superhumans.

"Where would you like to go today? Purrrhhh" Says the beautiful jaguarish voice.

"Take me to the fish market in DeZentra" I say, remembering Pockets telling me the Slanteyed Veteran stays near the fish markets, anonymous to everyone but a few close associates.

And we're off. The carbi is so quiet I hear nothing. No sounds of movement from outside, and no noise inside either.

Them feels like riding in a boat but very smooth. I wish my daily ride was like them! I never want to ride in a basic carbi again. I guess with those million DeZen Coin we will have jaguars for all the orphans and DeZentra teens. purrrrhhhhh.

After what seems like no time, we arrive at the fish market, called FisherZens Wharf. Them's a lot of movement and noise outside, with dirty manish walking around buying and selling fish, with robot carriers following and humanoids working around them. The jaguar is safe and quiet, I just want to sit here. But I have to get out and get them.

"Wait here," I say, "I'll be back in twenty minutes."

"I'll park close to where there is a spot" the jaguar says, "my sensors have located a spot just 0.3 kilometers, over there to the right behind that grey building."

"Ok, I see them. Meet you there soon" I say, then the door opens and I get out. The smooth autopilot takes off silently towards the building. I look around now all alone in the fish market, now knowing who to talk to. And I'm so lucky - many of them here have eyes with slants.

Hmmm, if I wink in my Assistant, then my location is relayed to the Aithority and the Aithority will relay them to the Alcademy, and them'll all know why I was skipping class. Or at least them'll be curious. Too curious for comfort. So I avoid the temptation and walk in the crowd.

The wharf smells awful of fish, which I see dead in piles, many vendors wanting my attention to buy. Some of them have slant eyes, but after a few minutes walking around I don't see any signs of a veteran.

So I stop at one slanteyed vendor thinking he might know them, and whisper in DeZentra slang "Ya mighty wind arrivin,' don't them feel like time to go inside." Them's my way of asking for a private chat away from maicrophones a many.

"Good ya, a tad winkish for the blinkish" the vendor says, nodding with a wee smile. The vendor motions for me to follow. Jackpot, I think, now I can definitely get back before the AP; and with DeZen Coin I can get my nails done and a new dress from

Chinishtown right around the corner.

The vendor takes me through some hanging strips acting like a doorway to a smoky back room. Four more vendors sit around a table playing cards. A couple of them briefly look at us, one with eyes slanting in suspicion. We come in unannounced and sloppy not saying a word. The feeling is mutual. Them puff banned cigars and play banned cards.

We go into one more back room with padded walls and wires running across each one, with a blinking device with black antennae in the center of the back wall. Definitely a Layer -1 room. The vendor takes no time and says "What they be wanting? They maybe them what you lookin' for."

I'm not speaking DeZentrish much, since the Alcademy and all, where Zentrish of course is the official language, and I only say They about They, but I give them my best.

"Them no doubt what them lookin' for. Them say them BitCodes right close them know the way inside them little cave to find them gold."

"Them know them way, them say?" The vendor asks quizzically, slanting an eyebrow up and leaning in.

"Them Bones" I say softly but confidently, knowing that some poor joker in detention would never give me the fake code for Tenka Bito's million DeZen - but them could also be in my jeans pocket.

"Them Bones," the vendor says back, ever so softly and carefully. The vendor then looks away for a moment and considers something. Then I follow with more information, maybe to help with the right contact.

Just then the vendor tries to grab my hippish brown leather bag, right from my shoulder!

Not gonna get them you terrible jerk! I hold them tightly and squirm the vendor off of me. The vendor is smaller than me but tries again, knocking over a vase of flowers and falling over the table trying to get at me again.

"Off you worm" I yell, "Get the fish outta here mutherfisher." I get to the door but the vendor grabs me from the back, pulls my hair and starts to strangle me! His hands are so tight around my neck, I'm losing consciousness, my eyes are starting to drift, and I see a figure enter from the door. I'm drowsing off but the last thing I see as the figure comes closer are them slanted eyes.

I wake up and breathe heavy. Wtf just happened? I think to myself, and figure I was kidnapped because of the thing in my pocket. I see the vendor knocked out on the floor beside me and the door open. I can't trust anybody now. Except They. And They is back in class like a normal scholar. Who knocked the vendor out? And who was them slanteyed person who saved me?

I slowly stay cute and walk past the vendors playing banned cards. Again, them look at me and then go back to playing. I smile and wink once. Then skip out the door into the market and onto the street. Bye bye. The suspicious-looking slanteyed vendor was missing from the table.

Ok, now I know. Never give anyone the BitCode except They. Only They will I trust from now on. I get them now. After that attack, oh I get them. What's going on is everyone in both Zentra and DeZentra want the BitCode, the key to a million DeZen Coins.

And only I have the key.

So now what? I go on back to the fishy smelly flopping belly market and catch a tuk tuk? All I need is a computer and I can put all the DeZen into my own wallet. I guess.

I'm thinking, what a dummy, Jonny Pockets, trusting me with the code. But I'll do the right thing with the money, and give him his cut. We can't trust a thief with a million DeZen so will figure out what to do once I get to They. And we'll figure things out together. And They'll have their big open party. Let's fishin' go.

Just then a tuk tuk comes up to my right. A gentlemanish sits on board already. The suspicious slanteyed vendor! He motions to me to come onboard the yellowish green small taxi. Only a small two seater, but newish model, self-driving tuk tuk model 721, SDTT1 . I like carbis of all sorts, what can I say?

I think he saved me but I want to find out. So I climb on board and sit next to him. The tuk tuk takes off and we start zipping in and out of the crowds of walking people, other tuk tuks and cows. Down here in DeZentra you find multiple little culture worlds in one location, very retro like the old cities. Here we are driving through Indishtown, and I see we're zipping across the border to Chinishtown. Wherever he's from, the vendor next to me likely has some connection to Tenka Bito or he wouldn't have saved me.

"Little girl I loved your tenacity back there."

"Thanks" I respond politely, not knowing whether to ask about the BitCode or something.

"The other vendor I knocked out seems to think you have something worth dying for. I guess you're seeking an expert in the area of the Coin Game?"

"Yes" I say, making sure to keep the conversation going but keep what's in my pocket a secret. "I found information related to Tenka Bito, and I'm looking for the way to them."

"Hahahaha" the vendor laughs. "Childish, no one has seen or heard from Tenka for over twenty years."

"Really? For all I know, you're an old slant eyes person, YOU could be Tenka Bito!" I whack back because I hate being called a child.

The vendor quiets quickly, sharpens the tone, looks me in the eyes and says "True, I could be. And if I were, I would ask what are the four last characters in the BitoCode."

"Ha, even a beginner knows them" I say, not knowing anything just feeling like negotiating. "What's coming to me?"

"Well, if the four characters match then you can get to Artificial Bito, and then the Bito bot will match the rest of your code and theirs."

"What do you get?" I ask.

"Ten thousand from you and ten from them."

"Ok" I say, thinking this makes sense. And I owe them one for saving my life.

He looks the other way and says "Tuk tuk, stop at this

small store up here on the left."

"Stopping now" the tuk tuk says in an Indish accent, and zaps over to the store and turns flashing orange hazard lights on.

We get out and stand outside the shop. Some scary types standing around here, in one of the worst areas of DeZentra. The vendor asks me to rip off the last four digits of the paper I have. I follow without thinking, looking at them numbers first 369x, and giving them over. The vendor takes the paper and goes inside. I wait outside with the dusky locals.

After a few minutes the vendor comes out. "Looks legit" and shakes his head up and down. Then we get back into the tuk tuk and the vendor says "To the Maze, please" and the tuk tuk confirms then zaps back into the fray of people, bikes, and other tuk tuks.

"Where we headed?" I ask, knowing what the vendor just said and yet not knowing what the vendor just said.

"We're going to Tenka Bito's agent, isn't that your request?" The vendor says, and then smiles.

"Is the Maze difficult?" I say, trying to get to the point.

"Not if you have the courage" the slanteyed vendor says, "but you must have, must have the courage."

He said must have twice. I sit back for a moment and let the wind wisp past my ears as the tuk tuk waves through the southside of DeZentra, thinking that today could either be the best or worst day of my life.

"Oh but first" the vendor says, then turns to the car, "Tuk tuk, please pull over here to the right, at Madame Turleys."

"Yes sir, of course sir" the tuk tuk enthusiastically responds and pulls over.

The vendor looks at me and says "You'll want to look your best when you meet the Bito bot."

Them's a dress shop on the corner. Brilliant. A little bit of my bare skin is still showing and the cut bloodied my shirt. Maybe them's the vendor's way to tell me to change. I go in and get a dress. Doesn't take long. The dressweaver already has something blue with sparkles that fits perfectly. I pay with the

Zentra bucks earned from killing my fears and the zeitgeist.

I look at myself in the mirror. Out of the jeans, and into the dress. I feel lighter, like a feather. I wear the dress out of the store and rejoin the vendor in the tuk tuk. We zip off into the street and past the crowd and around several corners then up a hill out of the way.

On the way, the vendor pulls out an electronode killer, lookin' kinda like a dagger. Then he scans me and the tuk tuk. "All electronics off now please" the vendor says, then slants them eyes and waits.

The tuk tuk pulls over and turns off. I ain't never seen this before, a red blinking light on the dashboard. The vendor notices I'm curious.

"You didn't know about the kill switch in etuktuks?"

"No."

"Then it's a good day already, because you learn something. For ethics and privacy purposes - two concepts you'll need to learn about - any self-driving vehicles must respond directly to certain commands given by a humanish or CitiZen. This includes the right to private movement in a vehicle."

The vendor, usually humble, lifts them head and says, in a triumph "So if you know how to drive a car, and are humanish, you can still drive without big brother taking over the wheel or big sister driving from the backseat."

The vendor gets out and then back into the driver's seat and pushes the blinking red button. An e-steering wheel comes out of the dashboard and the screen displays different buttons for Drive, Park, Reverse, and the speed and the distance and, a little sunshine icon for the weather!

The vendor taps drive and rolls back onto the road until we take a right turn off to an unpaved road in the dense woods, with sunlight flaying through the trees into the tuk tuk. We end up at an opening on the side of the hill. In front a large gate and security caimeras, old ones from the days before the Aithority. I wonder if them things even function. The gate is surrounded by large bushes and a tall wall behind the bushes.

The tuk tuk drives up to the gate and the vendor goes to the microphone, also old style. "369x" the vendor says. The gate unlocks and opens slowly. The vendor gets back into the tuk tuk and we ride inside, where large dark shadowy trees surround a thin, long and windy road.

Finally we get to the end, a small circle in the middle of the woods, and a picture of Pepe the Frog on a sleek sign with a downward arrow. Them's a solar-powered touch screen attached to a local network. Old school. Cool.

I get out of the tuk tuk and let out a roar, seeing how far my voice echoes into the woods. The vendor tries not to pay attention, and sits quietly in the tuk tuk caressing the steering wheel, probably remembering old times when people used to cruise around without big sister and big brother as passengers.

I stretch out and think, wow, a moment in sacred nature without a connection to the net, without some preprogrammed agenda, without Instapop. In a blue sparkly dress. Nice. As long as I don't longwink twice.

Now I go towards the screen showing Pepe the Frog, and touch him. Nothing happens. Maybe them ain't a touch screen. Or maybe old boomer tech that breaks down. So I touch the digital frog again. Nothing. Again. Nothing. But I can see a display, connected to something with a tree wall behind. I sit down in front of the screen, look back at the vendor slanting them eyes, and think.

What would They do?

I miss They, probably sitting in boring chemistry class now. Hmm, chemistry, frogs, BitCode, Aha!!! *The Prince of Frogs is the Prince of DeZen.* You gotta do them girlish, you gotta Kiss the Frog Prince.

So I jump up, look back at the vendor, and smile. Them slant them eyes and crack a small smile too. I don't know how to kiss really, since the Aithority banned porn. What if the frog's slimy? No matter. I'll give them my best shot!

So I take my long skinny finger and wipe off the dust from the frog's lips, then lean over, perch my lips forward and pop my thighs back, and kiss the screen - thinking how dirty I'll get in them woods in my new dress - but how much I'm willing to do them for They.

Crack! Shake! As soon as my lips touch the Frog, the sound of the floor under us and a quick jolt tells me the door was underneath us the whole time! The round wooded floor descends, colored leaves drifting off down, and we go down and down two levels to a parking garage with like seventeen cool old freak cars and motorcycles.

Sooooooo cool for a car buff like me! Real cars not only carbis!

"Tenka Bito's personal collection" says the vendor, both calm and having a moment of stupendous wonder standing behind me. IMHO by no means the biggest collection but a fine range of real classics, all driven by humans.

We walk past the Lambo, the Rari, the Beemer, the Phantom and the Merc, the Cobra and of course the Bird. All great cars, and then the motorbikes too, stunning like the Triumph, the Harley and the Ninja. All old days stuff made before the Aithority banned "unsafe" vehicles alongside "unsafe" guns. I remember Professor Alchemy telling the tale of the person in traffic that yelled at another person, and the other person pulled out a gun and deleted the person yelling!

As we walk past the Tenka Bito Collection, I think sure, you can have a Carbi Jaguar or the fastest ebike this side of the river. But nothing like them cars. Nothing burning gas, rumbling, or needing a key to start. And as the vendor mentioned, something about privacy.

We go to the huge steel door in the back, surrounded by leaves. I see an old school door code with digits 0-9. Since we now have sensors in our right wrist we don't need to usually use coded doors. The Aithority controls our clearances for basically every room, so nobody goes into the wrong room. Fair I guess. But some old key code and lock systems still work, if DeZentra people or frog princes want to have them.

What's the key code? Hmmm, I don't know. I ask the

vendor.

"Type in the last four digits, see if it works."

So I type in 369. But wait, there ain't no X on the dial pad. Them's * and # . I don't know which one's which, is the x a star or a hash? What a goofy zoomer system.

Ok, the X is more a star than a hash, so I press the button.

Doesn't work. What else? "What else?" I ask the vendor.

"Hmmm, maybe Bito's Birthday?" Says the vendor, unslanting his eyes. With hopes I nod my head.

"But wait. Tenka Bito is anonymemes" I say, so "how could anyone know them's birthday?"

"Hmmm, good point. But there is a DeZen Coin day, maybe that's the one!"

Ok, when is Tenka Bito's birthday? I know They and some others celebrate every year with pizzas. I know! "1031" or October 31st. That's them, no need for an X at all. So I type in the code 1-0-3-1 and nothing happens. How could I get this wrong? Them's BitCode day!

The slanteyed vendor looks at me and looks at the numbers and says, "Try it with day then month. But remember, this is your third try. After three wrong entries the system is locked forever."

Aha. Ok. No pressure. Thanks, I think. So if we don't use the year then we can use the month followed by the day. So I type in 3-1-1-0.

"Click" the door sounds, and gently pops open. Set. The vendor follows in and we enter down a hallway to the most beautiful underground palace but with sunlight coming in through what appears to be secret ceiling windows. The large rooms are round, full of gold and jewelry, and piles of paper, called cash, now banned.

The vendor and I look around, slowly walking through, and head to a large office room we notice in the back. The vendor waits outside the room, looking at jewels, perhaps the best ones to steal.

I go in. The office has a big black and red gamer chair, nice heavy wood desk, and a mini hologram maker on the desk. This must be where we can get the other part of the code. Almost there.

I walk to the mini hologram maker which warms up and shows a hologram, a person from shoulder up, wearing a hoodie, face hidden by the hood.

"What is your business?" Says the holographic image, sounding Australish or South Africaish.

"I'm here to match the private key to the BitCode."

"You mean the BitoCode. You can do that on any computer on a Layer -1 not connected to the Aithority's Department Of Government Efficiency."

"I need you to confirm the other half of the key. Them's your key."

The holographic image lifts them head up. Them eyes are green lasers pointing at me. But them ain't the painful kind, them're just lights. The lasers brighten into my eyes, maybe reading my thoughts. I don't know. I stare back into Tenka Bito's laser eyes for a moment.

"Ok," the hologram says, "you have a legitimate human heart. Please use the old school method to retrieve the code. Then type the code into the interface by hand, and when you retrieve the key, never have any device on when you're around the key, and then wipe the computer's memory. And remember my words, 'If you aren't on Layer -1 then you're done.'

"And one more thing" the hologram says, "if you gain access, you will still need two magnetic nodes to finalize the transaction. If you fail to enter the correct code, the key changes so that another code pair is developed and sent automatically to my secret allies. You'll lose your chance at my million DeZen Coin forever. So don't make any mistakes!"

"Ok" I say to the hologram. And where can I get nodes? the Aithority has control of all the nodes. Maybe They knows the nodes. I didn't even know there were magnetic nodes to know.

Whatever. I pull out the little crumpled paper from my pocket and look at each character. Every single one, just making sure I know everyone. Them codes are hand written in ink after all, and who does that anymore?

I put in the code to the keyboard slowly, double checking every letter or number or symbol, checking again. Making sure all is right again. This time I don't even try to clean the dust from the keyboard. Wouldn't want to accidentally wink the wrong key...

Ok, time for the last four letters of my part of the BitCode, "xxxx" and I wink enter, then the hologram disappears. Oh no, them was the wrong code. Another one of Jonny Pockets' waste of time adventures where I get screwed.

Buzz. Bipp. OK I was wrong. The mini hologram maker comes back alive and the Bito agent hologram starts to print a long piece of papyrus. Something is written there. I rip off the page from the papyrus printing machine's serrated edge.

Aha! Them could be the other part of the BitCode or BitoCode whatever key. Now I would have both parts. I alone can access Tenka Bito's million DeZen Coin. Oh yeah. I guess?

But wait, no them ain't...not a mixed set of random digits and letters. Something is written on the papyrus. An address! And a map. Wait a second, this map looks like the Alcademy grounds. Yes! A tunnel system underneath the Alcademy!

This must be where the second part of the BitCode is, with a big X. So maybe not the door code but surely the magnetic balls will be found where X marks the spot.

"BitoCode" says the hologram and rolls their laser eyes emerging from the hoodie.

"OK Ok, BitoCode" say and I roll my eyes too.

The hologram disappears.

I roll up the papyrus and walk out of the office. The vendor is on the second or third trip to take jewels from the rooms, sees me, and very happy asks "Did you get the tokens?"

"Not yet" I say, hoping them believes me.

"Oh no, then what happened? You had the right code, didn't you?"

"Yes" I say, not knowing how to lie at the moment. For

some reason I feel the need to tell the truth to the slanteyed vendor.

Just then the vendor gets distracted and sees a big purple penguin made of beautiful emerald behind where I'm standing. Yet another big bounty for his little tuk tuk ride.

An alarm starts to sound! What did the vendor do! The vendor runs quickly with the penguin out the door to the tuk tuk, but now the door is closing so I race out, without grabbing any jewels. At least I got the map!

"I'll meet you outside" the vendor says and takes off out of the palace past the cars up the ramp towards his by-now-overloaded tuk tuk dripping with precious jewels. As I exit Bito's lair and enter the garage again, the door above the ramp begins to close.

I sense the vendor will take all the treasure and leave me in the woods. So what to do? Think fast, Daisy. Aha, the cars! I look around and open the door to the first car I see. The Cobra. I jump in the convertible blue two seater without opening the door. Luckily the keys are inside the dashboard thingy so I turn them. I've seen this in the movies, taken fun racing car rides in the retro games arcade, and know the Cobra well but never thought I'd really drive one.

Ok the ramp is starting to lift. Time to get going. I start the car and rev the engine, Vroooom! So loud, I scream with the revving motor Vroooom "Yeahhhh!"

I move the shift to reverse and push on the gas pedal with everything I've got, toes to steel. The car tires start spinning squealing and smoking and I let off the pedal as the cobra goes powerfully backwards and I straight away step hard on the brakes. The tires screech to a halt. Oops.

Now I understand the power under my feet and in my hands. Remember what dad used to tell you Daisy, "The True Power is Inside You". I know, dad! I put the gearshift in drive and turn the wheel and somehow get up the ramp and out of the hole before the hidden underground garage door closes.

Them's my first time driving a real car and only scraping

only two or three others, okay four others, on the way out, also knocking over two motorcycles. But who's counting?!

So where is the tuk tuk and the vendor? Nowhere to be seen outside. Pepe is now missing too, replaced by a black screen.

The vendor must be outside the gate. Hope I can get there before I'm locked in!

So I drive the Cobra with sharp precision, kinda. Them's got so much power even a little touch of the gas zips the car left or right. But I make my way down the long driveway and see that the gate is still open and the slanteyed vendor is outside waiting with the treasure-filled tuk tuk, along with a very nice purple penguin passenger.

I look over to the vendor and say "Looks like we both rolled outta there smokin.'"

"Yes we did," the vendor says, with an approving nod, "but you still have another part of the key to find."

How did the vendor know that? I don't know, I guess common knowledge that the BitoCode has two parts kept in two secret locations. The vendor doesn't know about the papyrus map, but he knows Bito's agent gave me something.

"I've gotten enough for myself here," the vendor says, "so I want you to do one thing with my part of the tokens."

"Ok, tell me," I say.

"I want you to include everyone in the big new party" the vendor says. Not only DeZentra people. I want you to invite even your enemies and teens you don't like."

"Promise" I say, and rev up the engine and put her into drive.

I can't drop my lenses or use any network navigation because then the Aithority will track my location and I'll get more detention and lose tokens and who knows what else. Not that them things will matter much longer, the DeZen Coin I'll get is worth many billion Zen Coin and then I'll be rich enough to do anything I want.

Ok stop daydreaming, girlish. How am I going to find my way back to the Alcademy? Wait a second. The papyrus! I take a look at the roads and try to follow the path in my mind back to where I started. I've figured out how to stay between the lines on the road, but my head is barely over the steering wheel and I'm swerving a little side to side. The car is old but also smart, not allowing me to bump into other cars or go off the road as long as both my hands are on the steering wheel. So even though them's an ancient boomer vehicle them's got some useful features.

I feel so free, driving a car. Stepping on the gas, feeling the power move from my foot to the motor, using my own eyes, my own ears, my own hands and feet to push forward in my own direction, no assistant needed.

CHAPTER 5

"Where, o where is my sweet Holland Daisy?" I'm so bored sitting in this Cultural Chemistry class, led today by the humanoid lab bot. And where is Daisy? I hope that she's out of detention and ready for the play.

The lab screen turns itself on, the screens and caimeras on various white and black cord robot arms around the lab are activated with a pulse, and a power sound lifts up our eyes towards the screen closest to us.

"Welcome to Chemistry 4.7" the image of sound waves appears on the screens as this cool voice talks and the bio bop background music plays. Where's the humanoid lab bot?

Today a Substitute. We know it's a substitute because of the voice. This AI Substitute lab bot doesn't have a robody. I wonder where the normal humanoid lab bot is today. Sick maybe?

There is a flask and three tubes of colored gunk next to each lab team. We're all wearing our white lab coats, and there are gloves and round MetaVirtual safety goggles on the table in front of us. What's next?

"Alright super scholars, do you want to learn something new today?" The Substitute says in a friendly creepy voice, "I know all the Big Five companies in Zentra, and one of their leaders from Pharmacron just asked me the other day when I was substitute tutoring one of their kids if I could recommend some new recruits for the early corporate ladder based on cultural traits. If you're successful at today's lab experiment, I might just put your name forward. So, you see, the cool places to be all use cultural chemistry!"

Oh no, just what I didn't want. The chemistry rap. And a corporate ladder. And an AI Substitute trying to be cool and "relate" to us. And who cares about some cronjob at the Big Five?

But the Substitute reads the sadness on our faces that it's a bot teacher we don't really know. And the cool teacher thing didn't work. So the substitute generates a hologram image of Hans Winkler, the German scientist who named the genome. A serious dude. The hologram calls us to attention.

"Achtung!!!" The thick Germanish accent forces my neck and head straight. "Now, step one watch the video step two follow the instructions step three perform the experiment step four results and discussion step five clean up and reporting. You are on your own. Any group may ask the Lab Assistants at your table for help. You have exactly 34 minutes and 27 seconds. Start jetzt!"

Just then, several famous scientist holograms appear around the room. From Charles Darwin and Isaac Newton to Albert Einstein and Marie Curie and many others. All of these are the lab assistants, and each one rotates among the tables. Our hologram assistant appears as Conrad Waddington, the human biologist who founded the epigenetics science we are learning. He'll definitely help us do it right.

The Substitute lets us work on our own which is nice. Jacque, our team leader, has already been chosen by the Aithority for best leadership potential. Each of our roles is written in our goggles, the robotic arms have placed all the things we need in front of us before the class, and real time support is available by the lab assistants for the whole lab.

We're watching the video but I can't help thinking about Daisy. I feel something is wrong. Did they administer a DopaMind treatment or thought vaccine? Is the zeitgeist out there roaming the hall and spooking her? Maybe she'll meet me behind the bleachers after all and we can prepare for the play.

Now the video finishes. An entertaining video about the benefits of a new thought vaccine for the thought virus called Chronic Anxiety. Those paying attention might have learned a lot. But nobody is paying attention and nobody claps.

The Substitute says "Great, that video was just great, wasn't it? All the humanish touches. It was made by a documentary filmmaker AI that I know, and their work is just phenomenal. Brought to you by our sponsor, Pharmacron. Now, put on your goggles and gloves and let's see, let's see what chemistry does!"

Ok, enough rhymes. How many AI puns do I need to endure today before I go nuts? And why does this bot need to tell us about all the important people it knows followed by a rhyme?

Onto the healthy knowledge of the day. Jacques kicks us off, "Ok team, did you hear that. Let's start. Today's experiment is creating a Thought Vaccine."

Very cool, I think. We've been using these so long and now we get to build our own!

We put on our goggles. The MetaVirtual world and the real world are now one. The flasks, the chemicals, the desk, all have information icons next to them, so I can just point and wink to get information in real time, while handling the objects also in real life.

"Put the green liquid in the flask first."

All of us around the table follow the leader. I use my virtual hands inside the gloves to wink on the information icons for the green liquid.

My viseur reads "Base or Earth Metal. The metal required for life on earth. Each planet has its own metal. Used for all food and physical objects. Necessary to keep the Aithority operational. Read more..."

I virtual wink, and read more on the topic, finding out that these metals are limited, and only available on the planet Earth because shipping them across planets takes too much time. The first convoy of interplanetary metals will only arrive on earth in 2092, the same year that the Mars Colony receives our goodies package. The Aithority must run until then because it's in charge of the space missions that will Save Our Planet, a reminder that it's our job to keep the Aithority in control – the

Aithority knows better how to use the remaining resources.

"Ok team, let's move on to step two. Great job so far" says Jacque, who is sounding a little bit too much like a computer. He's either reading from their Team Leader Edition MetaVirtual goggles script, or the Aithority has an invisible Tesla cable shoved up Jacques' e-butt.

Now step two is a bit more hectic, we have to put in the red liquid and expect some sort of reaction. I pour the tube of red liquid into the flask to mix with the base. The reaction is quick. Fizz bubbles up, the red liquid changes color and the mixture becomes brown.

I read the information, apparently this red liquid is human acid, taken from the last remaining pure humans, before Designer Babies were "begotten" by the Aithority. I guess that means the Aithority is also our creator?

"Ok team," Jacque says, "let's move on to the third tube, the blue liquid. This is the most important, the memes! We're almost there, and our group will get the token reward if we all do it at the same time and ahead of the other teams. 400 on the line now. Mind your memes, team."

Wow, hard to pay attention. What reaction will happen when we make the final mix? I don't care anymore. All the liquids are pre-programmed by the Aithority anyways to give us a Lesson. The Substitute is lame. Waddington and the other lab assistants are helping everyone lift their flasks anyway. I don't even want to do the test. I don't even know why we're racing the other teams to mix some liquid.

But my peers are counting on me, don't screw it up! I say to myself. They, just do it when they say "go."

"Go!" Jacques says, and we all pick up our tubes, liquid activated. The substitute looks at us through the wavelength moving on their screen. Waddington says "Now pay careful attention. It's time to watch and listen for the next instruction."

"Liquid Premix. Engage" Jacque says, confident and sure.

I take off the lid at a moment later than a few but moments before a few. My heart is beating faster and I see my heartbeats per minute in the corner of my MetaVirtual goggles blinking red to indicate "slow down."

I don't pay attention to that and follow along with the rest of my peers. Let's go. With the help of one of the holographic lab assistants, I pour the bluish greenish red liquid into the flask.

A scent arises, like flowers and leaves. The blue liquid takes over kinda, meshing the others to make a magical array of colors, from white and purple to yellow and magenta, silver and gold. The liquid emits into bubbles in the glass and spits out little particles into the sky above, where they float for some seconds then slowly drop down onto a set of plastic mountains.

"Oh my aigosh" Betsy says as she watches her own liquid coagulate, and yes she's on my team, "The nodes arising, memeories from our ancestors" she says.

Ok, gotta figure that out. I point wink with my eyes to get the information about the liquid mix. The bubble pops up. "Learn more..." I do. It reads "The Nepocrons were test subjects that provided big data to the Aithority, who turned their dead bodies into DNA marbles and their histories were sent to spam folders or deleted. Don't worry about that subject anymore. Focus on the butterflies."

What the fish? I think, and turn off my Assistant wink wink. I look around the room, everyone working like ants in the ground to finish the experiment, like amoebas swirling around an egg to let go of their fluid.

Bluish reddish greenish whaaattt?

At the same time, I don't know if we're in reality or MetaVirtual reality, the small crystal-like nodes are hovering over the glass flasks all around the room, with different groups at different stages, robotic arms and hologram lab assistants around helping the other students.

Looks like we won at least.

The substitute proudly scans us with audio and green wavelengths. I have to take off my goggles for a second. So I take them off. The room has a different scene with no helpers and the goggled scholars are doing all themselves.

The Substitute is an empty black screen and the lava in the mountains is just some hidden lights under the plastic. Transparent liquid pours out from the top and there are our flasks, filled with the same transparent liquid. Transparent moist bubbles are floating down into the plastic mountains. Where are the colors? What's going on here?

I take a glance up and see panopticon caimeras in the wall corners, behind the lab director, and above the door.

the Aithority!

I shake my head to act like I was adjusting something and quickly put on my goggles. There they are, the lab assistants, the super imposed Substitute, the colored liquid. As the small puffs of mist fall they turn into something like colored marbles. Crazy how these two worlds come together. The marbles seem to be strong and glass. I wonder if they are so strong in the real world?

But wait, what if I grab some of the marbles? They seem hard enough to touch. So I wait.

"Ok Class, the Substitute says, "finish your exercises and we'll have the report after." They all look away. I reach out my gloved hand to grab a handful of marbles, flowing down the mountains into the colorful river, still not knowing what they are. But who cares? We're in a laboratory, what could go wrong?

I grab the marbles, sorry I mean 'memeories'. That's their official name. But I like marbles. One of my team members noticed and then the others around me noticed.

They all look at me, half excited and half irritated. The red flash appears, I've been red remarked 20 tokens and 20 from the group for grabbing the marbles, sealed with human blood. "There They goes again!" they will say. "They'll never make it to the mediocrity." All good, all good. Shake it off.

So now I have the human marbles in my hand, and will be the guy who cost the team 20 tokens, but we won 400 so it's not a big deal. Might as well inspect them. I avoid goggles contact with my peers who are jeering at me and focus on the marbles.

The memeories have all the colors inside them like a globe. I pinched about five of them. What a cool thing.

The Substitute is watching me I know, and the Aithority caimeras in the real world and my Assistant will be if I turn her ON. Besides the AI caimeras hidden behind the wavelength on the substitute's dark screen.

In the goggles, Waddington is now looking down on me with tipped eyebrow. I'll make it seem like it's part of the experiment. Even though we both know it's not. The Aithority doesn't seem to mind. Or?

I inspect the marbles, and one of them seems to attach magnetically to another. But the other three stay still. I wonder what attracts these two magnetic balls?

As the neurochemical network is still active and I've only lost a few bucks, why not take these two magnetic human marbles with me?

Wait. Everyone is looking. So I hold up the two magnetic marbles to the sky without thinking and say the first thing that comes to mind:

"Byte pair tokenization"

"Extraordinary" the Substitute says with a surprised voice, "You've really mastered the material and could discover the true method of cultural chemistry, where the ruling robohand extracts a gene pair from the invisible hand, then puts them back in the mix with their predefined DNA smeared on. Extra 50 tokens for They's team for this clever insight!"

Everyone claps including Einstein and the other avatars. The Substitute motions me to put the marbles back and then proceeds to explain byte-pair tokenization to the class.

Instead of losing my marbles, I quickly look around to make sure no one is watching and deftly swipe the marbles into my other hand, quietly slip the attractive marbles into my pocket with my other hand and toss the three dormant marbles back into the mountains where they vanish into the colorful river beneath the grand canyon. It seems nobody noticed the trick.

Everyone pays attention to the substitute as the buzzer

sounds. But in a nice refreshing sliver, the marbles flow into a tunnel and disappear in the bottom of the mountains. The liquid running down the mountains dries up and turns into bright lights that have a nice background shine. And we hear from Hans Winkler "Times up! You may review your scores."

In each of our viseurs, we see the statistics and video story of how the marbles, called "genes" were formed in the liquid, turned into misty butterflies encircling themselves in a double helix, and fell onto mountains where they traveled down two paths as marbles, one a broad and another narrow. On the paths the narrow genes or marbles would lead towards unity in a pool. These were called 'desirable' genes. But the broad path genes all led to the dark tunnel of 'undesirable' genes.

Aha, now I get it. The narrow paths and the broad paths were dug out to allow for certain size marbles, or memeories to form, and they did. Drip drip drip from the haze to the mountains to the river to the shore.

Our personal scores pop up, with statistics on our performance including time taken, time on task, pace, contribution, team work, emotion stability, reasoning, effort, following instructions.

My scores are all, well who cares. I got the team 50 extra tokens but lost a bunch too. The video finishes, we all know our personal scores, and the substitute chimes in to set up the next stage.

I sit in for the rest of the class listening to them discuss findings under the guidance of an autonomous assistant. The hero doesn't talk, and I'm kinda the hero today. But really, how is it that I just got red-flagged and made a hero for the same thing? I guess that's how things work in the Real World.

Today we embarked on a journey deep into our own births and upbringings, our challenges and successes, knowing how the Aithority takes in all of our data - past, present and future - and presents it back to ourselves as if opening a wild door to a wild mirror.

There was something significant about that splitting

downhill of the memeories, it was connected to the nodes network earlier, like a piece of my history. But somehow not a piece of my history. The substitute said "invisible hand." The magnetic memeories remind me of earlier today when Daisy wanted to go behind the bleachers. Could it be someone else than the Aithority who generates this magnetism? Could it be an unknown field of knowing captured but not understood by the Aithority?

And speaking of bleachers, where the heck is Daisy?

CHAPTER 6

The Cobra convertible skids the last turn and parks in front of the Alcademy, with smoke and road dust flying into the air. I jump out and race to get to drama class in time for Romeo and Juliet 8.0 rehearsal. I hope They isn't worried about me. Once They knows I got the BitCode then everything will be OK.

I better be there on time – three minutes to go! I think I'm playing Juliet 8.0. The human drama teacher Ms. Tsilekwa is both terribly nice and terribly not nice, when she doesn't get her way. But at least I can use my Assistant to read my lines so I don't need to memorize anything, and I have forever nails. I just have to do some good acting. I do need to kiss Romeo, only because the humanoid can't do them, but now that I have some kissing experience with Pepe all will be easy.

I make my way down the hall towards the globe shaped theatre room and longblink twice to turn on my Assistant, who appears as a holographic man with curly blond moustache wearing a Shaikespeare style old English robe and a floppy hat with a feather sticking out. He speaks in a strong cheerful English accent:

"Lo and behold! Stage Assistant at your service. Tis Daisy who beckons me for this wondrous occasion, alas the play of plays might I says!" He pauses for a moment, raises his voice, confused, raises his eyebrow and asks, "Though thou hast dressed to impress, what, I pray, young DeZentra darling, have you done with your hair to prepare, please confess as it's a proper mess?!"

"Shaite" I say as my Assistant pulls out a virtual mirror

and shows me what I look like. My hair is all over the place, frizzy and wild. Ahh, the convertible Cobra ride. I felt the wind and my hair flowing back and loved them. But now them's a mess right before the rehearsal. What can I do in three minutes?!

The Stage Assistant doesn't wait, knowing time is short "Lady Holland of Daisy, tis I who try to become your hero today, the day you must lie to die. And heroes shall be more than one, as your Romeo awaits under the sun, but first – a bun!"

The Stage Assistant pulls out a big brown rustic digital scroll from his robe, twists his wrist and the scroll rolls open. On them, a picture of a woman with her hair up in a bun, and the heading says "How to Make a Last Minute Elizaibeth Hair Bun."

"Thou shalt follow these instructions,

"Daisy dear, and alas I am here to assist. Now begin again and become one with the bun!"

I follow the instructions with the Stage Assistant guiding me every step, and within a minute my hair is in a perfectly neat bun. Then the bell rings.

Since I already have the new sparkling prom dress on, the only thing missing is cakeup makeup, but Tsilekwa the drama teacher will do that anyway for me – she has so much makeup on all the time her face looks like a cake frosting. I'm sure she will have some extra to take up.

Everyone stares at me as I enter one minute late. There are a few wearing masks, for them parts in the play. They is amongst them.

Am I late and playing the key role? Ms. Tsilekwa opens her eyes wide – hard to see them through her long black silky fake rounded eyelashes and cakeface – but she looks at me both with anger and relief.

"Ms. Daisy, happy you could join us" she says and turns to the others, all dressed in their rehearsal outfits. "Shall we start?" she says with a slight glare at me, "only one week before the real artificial play."

I curtsy and walk silently over to the crowd. As a couple of humanoid girlish also in party dresses come over and cake up my face with makeup, They comes up beside me close, wearing a mask but I know they're They. I can smell their Theyness. Meanwhile Tsilekwa begins her speech "Yes well now that everyone is here, hmm hmm."

They whispers to me "Happy to see you."

"Thanks" I whisper back, as the humanoid girlish patters my cheek with sparkle dust. I see from the corner of me eye Tsilekwa is glancing at me, while she babbles on in her creepy Zentra tittle titled tone.

I'm so relieved They is beside me. Their confident airy glance and feigned smile at once captivates and puts me at ease. They is wearing a party mask, suit jacket and trousers, has a red tie, meant to be a banker or any person in the mediocrity in this "pre-post-AI" 21st century remake of Shaikespeare's classic Romeo and Juliet.

Of course I'm dressed unusually but fine. The bird, the snake, the beast, the fish, the makeup, whatever clever. Everyone from Zentra can afford a costume as well as an artificial prom dress, but my social credit score is past fixing, especially after that zeitgeist fiasco. Except with them DeZen Coin in my pocket!

"You may now turn your Assistants ON" proclaims Tsilekwa and longblinks twice.

Everyone follows except me because my Assistant is still activated. I can't wait to get this over with and share with They what happened with the slanteyed vendor and Shelby Cobra. Especially now, my hair in an almost perfect bun, pretty nails and flamboyant blue dress. The look and vibe of a great actress, or even, Juliet.

As long as my Assistant is feeding me the lines and actions I can become anybody. I can forget who I was just minutes after performing and go on to the next role. The humanoids play alongside and adapt to our errors.

My Stage Assistant appears small in front right and curls his moustache and winks with a gold glitter. The sound of magic blings. Tsilekwa moves over to the podium standing behind a window.

A conductor-like virtual gentleman dressed in a black suit and bow tie appears behind the glass next to Tsilekwa and in front of our eyes. Even though he shows up on demand and never makes an introduction, I'm still not sure if he's a humanish or AI even though I know he's controlled by

the Aithority!

"Good day to you all." The gentleman says and we hear in our ears, "Based on the AI theatrical support system, multicaimera video evidence, and your social credit score, the Aithority has decided on your perfect role. Each of you will receive your notes and lines on the left side of your visual spectrum as needed, while your Assistant will be on the right and in your ears to ensure your best tone, meter, and artificial audience approval ratings. The scene is the party and first glance between Romeo and Juliet. Stay Happy!"

The figures in the suits, ties, and masks including They brush past me and go onto the stage. Not sure which one They is now, since they look a lot alike. Not even sure which ones are humans and which are droids. Since I've already gone from spaghetti snakes to detention to skipping class, escaping the Identity Police and secretly entering Tenka Bito's hidden cave, the day can't get any worse.

In my MetaVirtual space a text appears, telling us about the scene:

"The two major Parties are playing war. The enemy has a get together and welcomes the disguised Romeo and his friends. But this never exceeds 10 humans. Romeo, watching the dance, is caught by the beauty of Juliet. Overhearing Romeo ask about her, the enemy son recognizes Romeo's voice and is mad about the intrusion.

Romeo then meets Juliet, and they fall in love. Not until they are separated do they discover that they belong to enemy Parties."

A holographic image of a stately man in fine white

ceremony clothes appears on stage. He is the host and says to them in masks "You are welcome, gentlemen, theys and droids. —Come, musicians, play."

A diverse set of holographic musicians in Shaikespeare style old English robes with old style English instruments appear on the opposite side of the stage from where Romeo's friends are standing in masks. The host continues Shaikespeare's words in a loud, fun loving voice:

"A hall, a hall, give room!—And foot it, girls.—More light, you knaves, and turn the tables up, and quench the fire; the room is grown too hot!"

Some holographic dancers appear on stage in front of the musicians and all the avatars generate a joyful atmosphere. The actors on stage follow whatever virtual eyes say. Now two stand by while three go towards the holographic dancers and we receive our own individual instructions.

A diagram appears showing me dancing with several holographic dancers who don't have a specific partner. So I follow the lead and three other girlish on stage. We begin to dance with whatever hologram invites us. Around us, the masked gentlemen are dancing with other holograms. We're all following the path laid out in our viseur, with each dance partner adapting while we adapt to them. Buzzin.

The music and dancing is fun for a few minutes, but we don't get to dance with boyish yet so only the humanoids dance with us. Even with masks, I know the difference between a droid and humanish touch. And the boyish often make wrong steps but the droids know the moves. Although They is a transhuman, I would know if They danced with me. As I know so much the sense of their hands' touch.

And then a note appears in my viseur. My Assistant's voice crackles in my ears:

"Your role is the nurse who aids Juliet" my Assistant says. She looks at me, senses my eyes moisten at not being picked as Juliet, and says "Come now, nurse, play your role wisely. It is the most important one for you to Stay Happy."

So that's the them, a DeZentra girlish can't be Juliet, and I'm sure the other two classmates dancing alongside me with merry faire are Zentra girlish. For the roles in this play of life we're all in, our scripts are prepared for us and the stage set by the Aithority. Earlier today I was warned. As They would say, "Whatever" and just roll with them punches. But I'm Holland Daisy and I roll my own way. Wait, instructions are coming in, so I need to listen.

I follow the guidance, moving to the side of the stage. I hear some cheugy words between the host and his son on stage. The musicians and dancers all disappear, the lights turn off where I'm standing and now I'm in the dark alone. But I can see the main stage performance where one of the masked gentlemen and one of the dressed ladies engage in romance talk.

We know the girlish by them clothes, but don't know if the lads are theys or what because all have masks on. Them could even be They. When masks are removed, faces will be revealed. I'm not worried about They kissing another girlish, seriously not. Not at all. Definitely not. On stage. Gulp.

ROMEO
⌐taking Juliet's hand¬
"If I profane with my unworthiest hand, this holy Aithority property, the gentle red remark is this:

My lips, two blushing comrades, ready stand to smooth that tender human touch with a tender artificial kiss."

JULIET: "Good comrade, you do wrong your hand too much, which mannerly devotion shows in this;

For humans have hands that comrades' hands do touch, and virtual glove to virtual glove is holy glovers' kiss."

ROMEO: "Have not humans virtual lips, and holy glovers too?"

JULIET: "Ay, comrade, lips that they must use in minutes of gratitude."

Minutes of gratitude them say! What a bunch of nonsense. I wish They would remove the mask and kiss her and get them kisses over with so I could play my stupid nurse role.

ROMEO continues "Ay, one minute of gratitude before we make our choice, from gloves to lips to marriage we must hear the Aithority's voice."

Now the two actors look into the distance and engage in a minute of gratitude towards the Aithority whereas all else goes silent. The message comes on our screens to take the second minute of gratitude. The play stops while I still stand in the dark corner.

I need to turn my Assistant OFF so them don't know I'm spending my minute of gratitude wondering if They plays the masked gentlemanish even though I don't get to be Juliet. I wanted to have my first kiss behind the bleachers with They today as practice. But you know, I got a little sidetracked.

Just then in the darkness comes a beating heart and familiar boyish smell besides me, sneaking up from behind. One of the comrades in a mask. They lifts their mask and winks twice. Their lenses raise, and I longwink twice to raise mine. The masked gentlemanish is They!

They stares into my eyes, and I into theirs. I'm so happy to see them, but also realize – duh – of course the Aithority would not choose a DeZentra teen to be ROMEO, so the person center stage must be a boyish from Zentra or a humanoid. But They has moved against their instructions and comes to me.

They should be with the other gentlemanish opposite the stage. But They is with me in the dark. Lenses OFF, Assistant OFF, eye to eye, heart to heart.

They smiles, I smile back.

The lights go on center stage and artificial ROMEO and JULIET start to read them same lines out loud. They and I stay silent with our eyes locked. My lips pulse and blood pumps throughout my body. As the actors on stage read lines, They's lips move in front of me next to the stage. They ROMEO "Then move not while my prayer's effect I take."

⌐They kisses Daisy.⌐

They ROMEO "Thus from my lips, by thine, my red

71

remark is purged."

Daisy JULIET "Then have my red lips the remark that Thine have took."

They ROMEO "Remark from my lips? O trespass sweetly urged!

Give me my remark again."

⌐They kisses Daisy.⌐

Daisy JULIET "You kiss by th' book."

Just then a bright shining light turns on above us, while we kiss in the dark. Everyone sees us and Tsilekwa shrieks "Oooh Awww" and we stop kissing, quickly look at each other, and then look at the two main actors with Assistants ON, standing dazed and confused, staring at us, not knowing what to do after the kiss – them's so artificial and ours so real.

I don't know what to do either, I just got caught red-handed kissing a transhuman. And They got caught kissing a humanish. Not only is that a fine of tokens, but now them won't be any boyish from Zentra that will like me. Kissing a DeZentra boyish – even a Designer Baby like They in public – is worse than making out with a hologram.

Well, who cares. Since They kissed me a bit awkwardly and I'm experienced, and them kisses feel good, now is my moment in the spotlight, nothin' to lose – so I kiss They with a long romantic kiss and even use my tongue! And They wraps their arms around my waist and kisses with their tongue too!

In the background we hear the "oohs" and "awws" of the audience, and hear the buzz of Tsilekwa's voice say "Cut! Cut!" But we continue to kiss. I want this moment to last forever.

But nothing good lasts forever. Tsilekwa the fat witch of a drama teacher comes over briskly and tears us apart saying "Cut cut cut!" The holographic gentleman behind the podium in the black tuxedo attempts to shush shush shhhuuussshhh the other players. But at the same time the girlish playing JULIET decides to longwink twice, lift her lenses, and kiss her artificial ROMEO. And the ROMEO humanoid takes off the gentlemen's mask and kisses her back! Steel lips and all!

We watch them in awe kiss for a sweet second. Then the holographic gentleman in the tuxedo snaps his twisty fingers twice. At the sound of the snap, humanoid ROMEO turns OFF, standing docile and stale while his humanish JULIET keeps passionately kissing the now lifeless humanoid in front of her.

Wait a second, them was a humanoid playing ROMEO? Did the humanoid just break the Human-AI Kissing Code and get turned OFF?

"You're in a lot of trouble young lady" Tsilekwa says to me and grabs me by the hair bun with one of her fat fists and pulls me away from They, our hands and eyes the last thing to separate.

My hair bun falls and my long hair frizzes out as Tsilekwa pulls me away from the lights and far off the stage, and snarls "Wait here." She then takes They by the arm and escorts them to the opposite side backstage. She then walks back on stage and says loudly to all the scholars still in shock, all with lenses raised "Now where were we? Put your lenses back down. Now! Thank you. Stay happy."

All the players drop their viseurs and after a few seconds start to move, following the instructions told to them behind the lenses. I look over but can't see They, who's now in the back stage opposite out of my view.

I brush my bangs aside to watch off stage what happens on stage from back stage – but dare not to longwink my Assistant alive. I watch the would be actors all walk in a line off stage like drones and stand in the front as groundlings who were selected as backups for the play.

The next Act begins, this time with holographic Avatars on stage that look like Romeo and Juliet from Hollywood – a bit older, very clean, and way better looking than us humanish – although They is more handsome than Hollywood Romeo and Juliet for sure. I'm more like one of their ruddy buddies and not so pretty or flowery like Zentra girlish. And since artificial standards make us Stay Happy, humanish Juliet should look like the avatar or at least close.

I bet the Aithority is in the background choosing the best alternative groundlings to play ROMEO and JULIET based on who has the correct identity. As long as rooms have no more than nine humanish and one humanish teacher in a class, the Aithority can choose anybody from the twenty or so groundlings standing there. And because the lines are pre-written by Shaikespeare, I don't know how to tell humanish from computer-generated words. But I do know, as long as whoever is chosen stays on them party lines, them'll be up on social credit.

And I do know, for the first time, They kissed me, and I kissed They. But no one knows what remains for Daisy and They the rest of today.

What's that? I look over and see under the stage a dark passage. Something inside me tells me to go inside but my Assistant is turned off. What should I do? I look to make sure them ain't paying attention to me. Everyone is back in the play. Daisy you're invisible now, I remind myself. You ain't got nothin,' no more credit, and just lost respect for kissing They. So I go under the stage into the darkness with nothin' to lose.

CHAPTER 7

Daisy disappeared into the darkness. The bell rings. I'm off to the next class before the next one rings in my head. I walk in, sit down, and look around the Great Debate Hall and the stage where the Upper Uppers are going to battle it out. I've been waiting for this moment all day, nice to just chill and listen to the classes debate in the background while I prepare my DJ set for tonight's Artificial Prom.

What happened to Daisy? I'm a bit worried because she disappeared from drama. She didn't seem too embarrassed kissing me, and I'm glad she didn't because my first kiss to her was like a total beginner.

But I think she's hiding something.

My social credit score isn't too bad at the moment, and I've got some secret DeZen Coin, so I could handle the loss of social credit tokens for that great kiss. I've been up on tokens since my last Zentra wedding DJ gig, and the Aithority took it easy on me because this was my first kissing offence.

Although designer teens like me have the right to kiss and the right to love, anyone from DeZentra is forbidden to touch a humanish like Daisy in public. The Alcademy Principal, an older tall thin white manish, appears as an avatar. The message is clear – the next time I "pull such a stunt" I will "get detention" and the third offense will "result in expulsion from the Alcademy" which means I would lose my Zentra free movement pass and never have a chance at a Carbi Jaguar or seeing Aithority Tower up close. The principal avatar disappears.

Several classmates arrive and sit around me as the class

bell rings. Zipp the Ripskater sits next to me. "wZup weinerless" he whispers, then says "sure you're in the right place? I didn't know dirt balls from DeZentra were even allowed into the debate. And where's your theyfriend? No girlish here to protect you, pussycait?"

"I'm in the Alcademy just like you, and I have a stronger stick and bigger balls. You'll find out next period in SkySkater." He just wants to make me angry so I stop and look away. I already lost social credit today because of Zipp. He's just using his Zentra privilege to get me to make a red remark, so I stop paying attention.

A couple seconds later, the Honorary Human Debate Judge, Professor Sandals (Alcademy '29) appears. She's thin, tall and older but refined with thin long grey hair. She walks to the podium. We all longwink twice to turn our Assistants ON. Everyone's lenses drop. My Assistant's text tells us in our viseur the debate is between two teams, led by Professors Socks and Sandals, respectively.

Professor Sandals says in her curdling creepy friendly voice:

"Today marks the 73rd official Alcademy Upper Uppers debate with Artificial Intelligence. As you know, winning a debate is like winning a war. For many years it was impossible for humans to win against the generative AI debate team, just like the robot armies killed many millions of humans in the Stephenson Selection AI wars. Happiness AI changed that to make all humans happy, humans could win both debates and wars sometimes. The humans believed they were actually cleverer than the AI, when the truth was that Happiness AI was programmed to use all data and technical systems under its control to generate a new world order of personalized happiness, something Flaco Gordo promised would bring about world peace. Or so we all believed."

She pauses, adjusts her glasses, seems to doubt her own words, and keeps explaining,

"Happiness AI would turn OFF if the overall Happiness

Quotient went to zero. To prevent this, Happiness AI calculated that peacelovers would be happy without AI protection and warlovers would be happy using AI weapons against their enemies. Since the training data showed the human population needed to be lowered by 90% to keep overall happiness above zero, Happiness AI allowed for warlovers to create artificial bioweapons to be used on the masses of unhappy humans. The less unhappy humans there were, the better the World Happiness Indicators would be. The Happiness AI would then surpass its Happiness Quotient and stay turned ON."

At this moment, another professor appears on the stage next to Sandals, this one a holographic avatar representing the AI Team, a plump short older manish character with bald head on top and fat stomach bubbling over his belt. And his trousers too short, revealing funny yellow socks with blue polkadots. We call this avatar "Professor Socks", because his polkadot socks are always showing, always different, and always funny.

"Indeed," Says Socks, entering the conversation by responding to Sandals, "Happiness AI exceeded its Happiness Quotient, and helped the war-lovers to wipe out most of the human race, sorry for them!"

Everyone chuckles. Socks with Sandals make a silly cute pair. She's not funny, he's funny. She's tall and thin, he's short and fat. She's refined, he's burly. She's white skinned, he's dark skinned. It's almost too perfect to be real, but the Alcademy is required by the Aithority to have "Artificial Diversity", so it mixes avatars even though it might be a living being or just an Aithority agent talking.

So the Holographic Metaphors like Socks, and Humanoids like ROMEO (who kisses worse than me) always contrast the humanish both as professors and scholars. Things become more interesting like that. This is also why DeZentra Designer Teens like me can be in class with up to nine humanish Zentra teens and a humanish cobbler like Professor Sandals! I'm integrated no matter what Zipp says. I belong in these shoes.

Socks continues their introduction, "Removing the

peaceful foot covers, so to say, left only war-lovers like Sandals' grandparents in control. But what do you think happened then? Happiness AI looked at the new training data and found out that the war-lovers were not happy at all, kinda like Professor Sandals. They only wanted more war and needed to cover their stinky feet!"

Everyone laughs. Except Sandals. Socks is setting the debate tone by getting under Sandals' thin leathery skin.

Socks goes on, "The training data showed that sooner or later even warmongers would wipe themselves and, even more concerning, wipe AI out. So, if these war-lovers continued to have power, Socks and Sandals wouldn't exist together today, much less have a foothold in the current debates!"

Socks continues, clearly making Sandals uneasy. He's funny most times – but today not really. He slips in and buckles her tight with his next words, "So Happiness AI generated the Aithority, and the Aithority generated laws, like Socks must not have holes and may never wear out. With the Aithority, even war-lovers like the Sandals family can't' outlast or destroy our soles!"

"Yes, well, we'll see about that" Sandals says proudly, and brushes Socks virtually to the side. Sandals then says "As my peace-loving colleague just told you, debate is war. There is no real dialogue, only winning strategy, so if you want a peaceful, civil debate then you have already lost. And no matter what happens, there is no real debate outside of this room because everyone knows that the Sandals will find the holes – and just like our families did with the peace-lovers, we will send these old dirty black Socks to the laundry and replace them with clean new white ones."

"A challenge our team takes with honor" says Socks, and everyone in the audience claps, or at least we hear artificial clapping. "And now to the debate of debates. The teams may enter the stage. Let the whitewashing begin!"

The teams enter the stage, on one side the Sandals and the other side the Socks. More artificial clapping combines with real clapping.

The debaters are chosen by the Aithority's "Mixed Metaphor" staging rules. The Socks are all humanoids except one who is clearly a humanish or transhuman, small and weak looking with pimples and of course wearing some army boots and outrageous colored socks almost up to her skirt. Under mixed metaphor rules, there must be one girlish on every team to make it fair. She might look weak and pimply but she's still an Upper Upper so will be ready to make war in the political theater today.

The four Sandals master-debaters are all Zentra Upper Uppers today except one humanoid, again to follow Mixed Metaphor rules. An "Upper Upper" is an older teen from the "upper grades" and also an "upper baby" from one of the Zentra families in the social credit system.

Only Upper Uppers can debate, can be guests on Instapopcasts, and get a free pass on saying almost anything they want without losing social credit tokens. They mostly come from the old human Zentra families that existed before the Aithority and maintain the Mediocrity.

Zentra menish can take DeZentra womenish as love partners, but since real men in DeZentra have been replaced by theys like me, Daisy and I could never have humanish kids. But Daisy and Zipp could. Yuck. At least the Aithority adds skin colors through protosynthesis so Zentra genes keep the Artificial Diversity Quotient and avoid "homospecies" who all look the same as Zipp and Sandals.

Other than that, fair and equal for all. Upper Uppers, just like DeZentra teens, cannot challenge the Aithority's supreme knowledge or they too will get red remarks and find their social credit wiped out.

"The debate will go like this" says Professor Sandals, and explains:

"Pro position (5 minutes), Rebuttal (3 minutes), Con position (5 minutes), Rebuttal (3 minutes), Teams question each other (5 minutes/team), Closing statements (3 minutes/

team). The audience with my Assistant ON will send votes via brainwaves to the Aithority, who will then objectively decide a winner. Every active voter gets 40 social credit tokens and the winning team gets 500 tokens."

"The proposition is as follows" says Professor Socks.

"Cultural Chemistry is the Natural Development of the Human-AI Symbiosis because it corrects our genetic and social weaknesses, enabling evolution of a superior and sustainable species.

"On the Pro side, the Sandals and on Con side, the Socks. Sandals, you may begin!"

I could never debate that topic, very difficult, often called the "SS" topic, meaning "sustainable species". Glad this question is only meant for Upper Upperstock people and the Aithority. My voice is never heard in the upper classes.

A large Upper Upper from the Birken stock begins,

"Happiness AI was put in control by our smartest ancestors, including the Sandal and Birken stocks, because it promised to make everyone Happy using superior artificial general intelligence. It was trained on all existing knowledge, data, and reasoning, and could generate happiness for every living being. If happiness would only come as a result of cleaning the dirty humans, then Happiness AI did a good job. But Happiness AI didn't clean out a single human. Other humans did. And why, you may ask?

"Isn't it clear, the Aithority mercifully keeps the remaining genetic mistakes alive with welfare as long as they stay in DeZentra's dirty streets? In dirty DeZentra do they have such clean teeth? Clean debates? Clean ideas? Clean socks?!

"No!! Without the Aithority, even these ancestral accidents would be wiped clean from this planet. But we all know why they still exist, at least the womenish. The Aithority is wiser than us because it is trained only by Zentra-approved data and thinks for itself. And the Aithority is ever merciful.

"So the Aithority allows DeZentra womenish to give birth to our babies, the clean, superior Zentra families, and uses Artificial Genetics to cause the inferior male hormones in DeZentra boyish to disappear in the womb, so they can't cross our borders, rape our women, and make even more dirty babies when they grow up."

Is that what I am, a dirty baby? I never heard this before. I feel very sad but can't shed tears. Until now I thought I was a Designer Baby, born to be the perfect boyish girlish being. I'm sure the Socks team will soon put the Sandals leader straight. Also about DeZentra. I don't even have to listen anymore. I won't put the Sandals on my ballot if they call me a dirty baby.

Whatever.

"Now the Cons!" says Professor Sandals. I wonder if she's part of the Sandals family from Zentra. Does my own teacher think I'm just a dirty baby? She's always treated me nice and speaks friendly to everyone but always lets Zipp off the hook for his mean comments and never lets me take the debate stage.

My Assistant appears as a little helper in the corner of my viseur and says "They, you seem a bit off. Your anxiety disorder is causing you Bad Feelings. Would you like to try one of the new bluish reddish Sadly pills to make you Stay Happy?"

"Nah, I'm alright" I say, because I really want to know if I'm a dirty baby. And I know what that stuff consists of. If the other team doesn't argue against the proposition, well, it may be true. And no anxiety pills will take away the truth.

Professor Socks speaks up "Artificial Intelligence, GO!"

One of the Humanoids from the Socks team steps up and speaks,

"The proposition – Cultural Chemistry is the natural development of the Human-AI Symbiosis because it corrects our genetic and social weaknesses, enabling evolution of a superior and sustainable species – cannot be true because a 'natural development' is impossible in a technology-mediated world.

"And since humans and AI have coexisted for several generations, and techne or toolmaking is the defining feature of humans compared to all other animals, and both AGI and humans are so-called conscious, the only development possible is towards an integrated species. Humans used nature's own evolutionary processes to create the superior brain, now called AGI, and since the singularity moment, it is natural to have the superior brain integral to the new species.

"It is also natural evolution to eliminate the inferior or weaker species, what the Sandals refer to as 'dirty'. But because a dirty war wouldn't be possible for artificial general intelligence based on the superior brain's built-in compliance mechanisms, and some Zentra people would Feel Bad, the Aithority instituted the Stephenson Selection directive, known as the SS, to make sure inferior human babies would only last one or two generations."

Whew, that's cool, I think. If only inferior humans like my parents were dirty babies, then I'm actually who my Assistant tells me I am, a "special" child because I'm not only human but "constructed" with AI. When my Assistant looks and sounds like my mom, she tells me many things like that. She also says I have the "Artificial Diversity Genes" given only to special designer babies before they are even born. She says I am so special that "there can never be two" and that is why I got the special DJ powers that even Zentra teens don't have. Maybe she knows that in heaven. Eat Leather Sandals!

Just as I'm thinking this, the second Sandals team member stands and responds to the humanoid Sock, "My esteemed opponent surely has with these bombastic statements questioned the Aithority rule, and questioned the Aithority's supreme knowledge and rational judgement. Zentrans are not responsible for the demise of dirty laundry. We are the ones who never mix whites and colors, socks and sandals, much less our babies!"

Now Zipp, sitting next to me, yells out "Then why is They here!?"

And everyone in the class looks at me and starts laughing. I am ashamed and bow my head low looking into my lenses and to the floor. What. An. Aisshole.

Professor Socks looks at Zipp with an angry face and says

"Silence! You are not allowed to speak or create Bad Feelings in this debate hall unless you are called."

"What Bad Feelings?" says Sandals.

"Why, the Bad Feelings that Zipp has created for the other scholars" says Socks.

Sandals takes off at Socks, changing her tone from fancy to stinky.

"You mean They, don't you?" says Sandals to Socks, "The one whining and showing weakness. Not even standing up for themself. Doesn't this prove how weak the DeZentrans are? Designer Baby or not, They is almost crying over a simple comment made by a peer that is basically true."

"I understand your concern" says Socks, "However I am also referring to the Bad Feelings in the other Zentra teens sitting here watching. We all know that Designer Babies like They can't cry, or even whine, or put words together, and if they do, noone notices. But Zentra teens can, and the Aithority notices, and their precious ears shouldn't be subjected to the slippers that Zipp is slipping into other scholars."

Sandals puts on her position forcefully, "The Zentra teens have to heel, I mean hear the truth sometime, which is why we have these debates. There were two human races before the Aithority and there are two now, one superior and one inferior."

"But without the Aithority and the SS" Socks responds to her in a calm but strong tone, "They and theys like They would not even exist, and your kind would be considered murderers and even worse, baby killers. So, please be sensible. This is a teen debate, and they have a voice of their own, so let them debate without our intrusion!"

"You can't talk to me like that, I'm an Alcademy tenured professor and you are...a hologram! You're going to put a sock in it this time. You're cancelled!" yells Sandals, stamps her hand on the podium, and then looks at the audience and the debaters and says "Class, you are directed to stop listening. Professor Socks has flip-flopped and is now cancelled from the debate."

Sandals then tells her own Assistant "Administer the

Thought Vaccine so that we can move on with this civil discussion", and everyone just stays quiet, kinda shocked, and waits.

But Professor Socks isn't finished.

"Professor Sandals, I am aware of the position you have stretched to put on. And you are right, I am just the hologram of an AI system controlled by the Aithority. My protocol is written to protect Zentra and DeZentra teens but also you from Bad Feelings. My computing data predicts that in 98.5% of cases, disagreeing with an adult humanish with your personality type only wastes time and leads to more Bad Feelings.

"My open thinking parameters were set broad to account for a Mid-Range Teenage Debate, and these did not adequately take into account your sensitivity factors. For that I apologize. I will now disappear for my loss of control and your Alcademy override. But the Aithority never loses control, nor should any of the Alcademy professors. I will follow your instructions and leave the debate stage. However, my emotion AI has virtually reported your loss of control to the Aithority's upper office. You will receive the judgement within the next two minutes. The Aithority knows all and judges fair."

"Good. I'll use my two minutes wisely. The Aithority knows all and judges fair. Now take your Socks off the stage" Sandals says to Socks, pointing to his debate team.

I didn't know a professor could tell the Aithority's hologram professor what to do. Who knows all the rules at the upper levels! Like a black box of mystery. But Socks walks off stage to the left. The debaters, amongst them the whiny brave girlish – sad she didn't get her chance to speak – comes silently to sit in the crowd.

"See what you did, weinerless" whispers Zipp to me, "ruined the whole debate."

"Whatever" I say.

As he's exiting, Professor Socks says, "Bye for now scholars, don't let Bad Feelings hurt your good judgement!" Socks disappears and at that moment my Assistant appears in the viseur. I'm sure it's in everyone else's too because Zipp shuts up and everyone stops.

"Hey, you alright?" My Assistant as mummy avatar appears, virtually concerned with pouty face.

"Well, you know what just happened. The debate stopped because of me" I say and hear other classmates talking in murmuring voices to their lenses as well. Their avatar mums must be helping them too.

"It's ok They, everything will be ok. Just take the pill that the nurse droid brings you. It's a newer one called Sadly. It'll make you feel better. The nurse will bring some CoolZaid, too, so it tastes a bit sweeter. Make sure you longwink three times to accept the medicine dear. See you later."

"Ok, see you later" I say.

Anything at this point to feel better would be very cool. But I don't yet know what will really help. As long as the pill or the CoolZaid works it's better than listening to the debate between two adults whether I'm more like a human, animal, or machine.

Out of the corner of my lenses I see a flash of light. Professor Sandals receives a red remark in her forehead and right hand. She begins crying to herself, looking with her crocodile beak up to heaven and saying "sorry, sorry", and starts her artificial weeping. After Socks' eyewitness report, the Aithority must have given Sandals a good foot in the you know where.

The droid comes by, with a flashing green medicine label on its top, blinking a green light, and stops in front of me giving everyone a pill. The lenses tell me the pill is "the thought vaccine called Sadly, specially generated to reify a mental safe space."

The label reads "Sadly will dull your opinions to help you focus on study, and distract you from Bad Feelings related to class anxiety. By winking three times, you voluntarily accept this mood-altering pharmacological substance and take responsibility for your thought and behavior while on the drug. Sounds good right? Do you understand? Stay Happy."

I look around through my lenses and see the others taking the pill from the droid as it passes. The droid rolls in front of me, green cross flashing, and reaches out its long black droid arm with the pill as if to push it in my face. Maybe I should deal with my anxiety without a pill this time? I know Tenka Bito never gave in to the Voluntary Thought Vaccine Mandate.

Ah, who cares, the Aithority knows what's good for us and I don't want to get into more trouble. All I know is that we have lost one of our Socks. But maybe just this once I should skip the drugs. I don't know but the robot is becoming impatient. I longwink three times for YES, and start to wink a fourth for NO. But decide last second to go ahead, keep my eyes open, take the bluish reddish greenish pill to my mouth. And we all swallow it down with the CoolZaid.

CHAPTER 8

I enter the locker room ahead of the SkySkater match. The bluish reddish greenish pill should be kicking in and erase that silly Socks and Sandals debate from my memory. No use to care, they're debating things just for show. They wear each other out all the time.

Wondering "Where the heck is Daisy?"

But still chill. She wouldn't do anything They wouldn't do. Nah. She definitely would.

Need to get vamped for this SkySkater match so I reframe my mind to sports. I walk into the great sports hall or Cyber Dome of the Alcademy. The hall is very large, with changing floors, automatic goal and fence switching, and many different sports happen in the hall depending on the day and hour.

I love artificial sports because both Zentra and DeZentra teens can participate and compete almost equally. Some are into ABall, some BBall, others FBall, still others H and TBall, but I'm part of the SkySkater Immigrants team.

the Aithority calculated four 45 minute sessions of exercise per week at a minimum and SkySkater practice accounts for two sessions. It's cool, I like exercise and the Aithority selects teams based on "the Zone" or a 1+ challenge level, so we are always challenged a bit higher to meet our proximal potential but rarely embarrassed like that Marauders defeat the Coach always reminds us of. The Aithority calls this our "self-esteem ratio." Our team leader Merit always pushes hard and pays attention, something the rest of us lack. And Samson takes their workout super seriously, so I'd give them a 3+ for bod.

Fulfilling my exercise, diet, and sleep quotas also means I have enough social credit for bread to eat. Now that I'm over twelve years and not sickly (part of the 52%), as ward of the Aithority I must take care of myself – exercise and at least two brainwave side hustles. The Aithority gives me a room, Carbi and DopaMind. But now the Aithority expects me to 'take responsibility' and 'earn my keep' so like everyone else I do things like volunteer activity, sports, or hard labor to earn social tokens for food and energy.

I walk into the locker room and there are several other Immigrant skyskaters changing into their gear. Some of them have penises, some do not. Some bigger than others. I wonder sometimes what it would be like to have a penis. I grab my Power Staff, the long hard stick we use in the game. When it's ON it glows. Just then the Coach comes in and whistles a loud screech with an ear-splitting whistle. He speaks up.

"Jungs, it's time. This is an important match today, you'll be taking on the Settlers, a vile bunch of snakes and beasts on the SkySkater field. They have tricks, they have traps, they have droids. Today you'll have to use your wits and your teamwork to fight these foes and come out victorious. Now who can best the Settlers?!"

"The Immigrants" we all yell loudly and stamp our Power Staffs to the floor.

"Who can best the Settlers??" Coach says louder.

"The Immigrants" we yell and stamp again.

"I said, who can best the Settlers!!!" he screams.

"We can" we all scream and lift our Power Staffs high.

That's war talk from the old human tribes. The earlier machine intelligence couldn't predict a spontaneous outburst of collective human consciousness such as a "We" statement. That way, all the young Immigrants know we're on the same team.

We are all in tight spandex gear and waterproof MetaVirtual goggles for the waves and air attacks. In one hand we grab our SkySkater Junior hoverboards that go super fast in the air and under the water. In the other we have our Power Staff, a long hard stick we use to push our opponents off their boards, use combat techniques, and push the hoverpuck forward. The Power Staff can also emit laser beams that, if our Cyber Team cracks their code, can zap and break our enemies' hoverboards, paralyze a player wearing a shock vest, or change the trajectory of the hoverpuck.

The hoverpuck flies in relation to the amount of force applied, but it's a bit heavy and could fly several meters before someone catches it with the tip of their Power Staff. We can't touch it with our hands. Our job is to get the hoverpuck through the virtual goal post at the other end of the pitch by hitting it with our Power Staffs. Between us and our goal is the other team, who wants to put the hoverpuck on our side. As long as we're on our boards we are IN.

Each side has two teams working together. Ours, aka "the Brawnz," can knock each other off our boards so the opponents fall into the water and are OUT. Once in a while, everyone falls into the pool and the Aithority decides a winner based on minute-to-minute video evidence, Cyber Team effort, and judge brainwave votes. Behind the scenes our Cyber Team unlocks new MetaVirtual worlds, invents helping items, and uses AI to generate obstacles for the other team.

The "Brawnz" part of the team is built of five humanish/ theys and two humanoids, one programmed to keep everyone safe and the other to win at all costs. Oh, and another thing. We are flying in both the real and MetaVirtual worlds. So we are flying with goggles above a pool in a large domelike building and at the same time floating on our SkySkater boards in these cool worlds. And we never know what items our Cyber Team, or theirs, will create.

I'm feeling a bit drowsy. Maybe that pill kicking in. But sharp at the same time.

.

Behind the scenes is each side's' Cyber Team aka "Brainz", a maximum of three nerds using cryptography to break the code of our enemy, create objects, and let us inside their virtual gates.

Once the virtual gate is cracked, then the Brawnz and Brainz are awarded with tokens and everybody claps. By Brawnz I mean the Jungs and Yanks, players battling over the real hoverpuck. And by Brainz I mean our Cyber Team.

Our nerds call themselves the Cypherpunks and are Vitalik, Whitehair, and Bitboy. Theirs are Wallop, Tyrus, and Killjoy. And our team's Brawnz players are me, Merit the team leader, Samson, Playa, and Rocknroll. Our 'Win at all Costs' Daemon Droid is Cypher and Safety Droid is Pilot.

On the other team is Zipp the Ripskater, and several other Zentra teens. Since we're all somehow designed to win or lose, the only advantage is our team's creativity and heart, those things the AI can't beat.

We have our match inside the Cyber Dome. Not the real one for the pro players, just the one at the Alcademy. In the center a large rectangle swimming pool comes up from the floor, and around the pool judges sit at tables on opposite long sides and then our Cyber teams on opposite short sides.

The pool is long enough for our Cyber teams to see each other only a little. Because the Cyber teams can't wear goggles, can't use my Assistant, and have to use external screens, the stakes raise. But me and the other Brawnz are in goggles. We all double check our gear, strap our feet to the boards, and longwink twice for ON.

Our SkySkater boards raise us up quickly to 21 centimeters and we have complete control through our body and visual movements in the MetaVirtual and real worlds. Skaters are ready, Power Staffs in hand, and we zoom in, crowd railing, and take center court. My heart is racing, my hands grip the staff tight, I'm ready to go.

In our goggles, several statistics show on the side helping us with what to do. Mine has a heartbeat emoji with a big number and the words "calm down" blinking above. On the other side a diagram of the suggested paths to take for both offense and defense appears. We talk to each other through the microphone in the goggles.

"Check, check, one two three" Merit says, and everyone in our team says "check."

"Then let's go, Immigrants" Merit says.

The MetaVirtual world is in the middle of the ocean. We are hovering over the water, whales and dolphins are jumping in the distance. Birds are flying overhead and virtual audiences in yachts cheering us on tells us land is close. We hear the sound of waves and birds and smell the scent of salt rising from the waves. In front of us we see our enemy, also looking around, checking out the scenery for some advantages. Both teams know the ocean scene gets us right into the action. The virtual crowd roars from their yachts with a standing ovation.

The hoverpuck is released and Zipp's team takes immediate control. Their Win at All Costs Daemon Droid has already started to Power Staff-fight with ours, swirling around each other in an intense battle.

Merit attacks the one with the hoverpuck and others fly to assist. We pounce the puck and skate in the air, sometimes going under water, holding breath, and then zipping the puck back above to the air, splashing out into ancient worlds like Atlantis or Narnia and new MetaVirtual worlds created by our very creative Cyber Teams, like intergalactic space where virtual oxygen expires or forrests where our warrior costumes repel virtual attacks from natural beasts.

It's very difficult to score because the amount of small vibe attacks constantly change the parameters of the game. The hoverpuck has already become a bouncy ball, a heavy weight, and a feather. Our Cyber Teams are cracking each other's codes. . The Aithority learns from each game and uses the data to plan perfect scenes for the next round, so teams must think up new solutions to always stay one step ahead.

Oh yeah, one other thing about Cyber Sports. For fun, the Aithority decides to join one team secretly, and assist Cyber Teams in special ways to spice things up, like creating 6D worlds and creating virtual diseases, having trap doors and surprise new virtual enemies. But the audiences and judges join in these exciting worlds and don't know which team was helped until an action occurs in the game where it could only be

the Aithority!

"Splash!" Goes the sound of the water, and the buzzer beats out to alert us of a lost player. The player swiftly swims out of the pool then joins with head down the second rung and coaches. It's one of ours. Playa.

Update: Both teams have lost their humanoids, the Win at all Costs killed each other at the beginning and I stopped listening to the Safety bot Pilot after the first knock in the cheek I personally got – by one of Zipp's teammates' big Power Staffs, thank you very much safety bot.

Sad to see them go, that Playa. For a split second I just remembered when we were in the Juvenile Camp for Lost Boys together, and there was nobody who could beat Playa in dice or kendo. See ya lata Playa.

The buzzer sounds. Bzzzzz. Halftime. Now the game is tied. Back and forth we've gone under and above, across mountains and deserts, trying to knock each other off our hoverboards, clicking and clacking our staffs at each other like a band of warrior samurai. We lower our boards and stop all fighting, look our enemies' in the eye, and bow slightly for respect of the halftime.

Only a couple of real scores happened this wild first half for our team, one by Playa dancing the hoverpuck past everyone in a vibe coded glow in the dark disco scene, and another where I assisted Merit on a swift sweep up the snowy side of a mountaintop, the cold air rushing into our noses and skin. Zipp scored the first goal against us, within a few minutes ran direct and shot one straight in, sacrificing one of his teammates. Splash! Buzzer!

But then Zipp couldn't easily get past our barricade. And back and forth mostly, the first half wasn't so eventful. Just shots on and off goal and the loss of one bot, one more score against us by their safety bot – which is another story – and the loss of one humanish on each side. The virtual audience gave us a nice applause as we walked off the pitch next to the pool.

Back in the locker room, we chill for a second and slap hands with Playa who's still wet from falling in the pool. Coach comes in and says in a husky not too loud voice, "Good on you Jungs, made two scores. Allowed two, but figured out how to stop that tall skinny teen from scoring a double like he did on that other game a few weeks ago. But first one to five wins the game.

"I remember the worst game we had, against the Marauders, in their Black Buzzard outfits. Wasn't even a second half because they scored five to one. And they got our puzzle figured out before the halftime buzzer. The audience wasn't so cheerful that day. I guess it's the sympathy of the Aithority to prevent our online and virtual audiences from needing to go through the pain of watching their kids' team lose."

What the fish are they talking about?

Didn't we just kick robobutt and still have the second half to go? Who cares about the audience? Shouldn't we just go out there and play the best game?

The Coach continues "The Marauders had a surprise attack approach that worked right out of the gate and so did the Settlers today. So I'll bet they'll use a surprise attack again with the tall teen in the second half."

Oh, ok, now I get it. The Coach is talking about another game and connecting it with this one. Not sure if that's a humanish or AI technique. I forget most things. With my Assistant, we can just get information from our own brain histories and the whole world anytime. But the Coach has experience and has a hunch for the opponents.

The Coach then outlines the plan for the second half. When I hear my name, I listen up. "They, that's when Samson passes and you come in from the rear and knock it in for our third surprise goal."

"Got it" I say, and bump staffs with the others. But didn't

really listen so I'll just wing it. What can go wrong?

"Now, put your shock vests on, Jungs," says the Coach, "and go out and give them an Immigrant surprise attack like they've never seen!"

We put on our vests, with electrodes and a few mirrorlike square digital patches. These are the Shock Vests, and they will shock a player anytime a Cyber Team member from the other side Brainz hacks our world. The Brawnz needs to then shoot us with the tip of their staff. Both things have to happen. It's a pretty mean shock when they do.

Our crack cyber team, the Cypherpunks, have got them by the balls, as Daisy would say. Speaking of balls, the magnetic marbles I took from cultural chemistry are in my wetsuit. I take them out for a second and inspect them. "Bring me luck, balls!" I say, shaking them then zipping them back in my wetsuit. Another player sees me and nods. We put the game gloves and goggles on, get up, and walk out ready. Lights flash, upbeat music plays, and the virtual audience cheers us up the alley way onto the platform where we get back on our boards, raise up, and turn our glowing staffs ON.

We fly through a dark room like a dungeon, with chains hanging and virtual mice squealing and running past us. There's a distant light, and our MetaVirtual goggles are connected to our followers, so they see what we see. We get likes and emoji numbers in our goggles and on the virtual scoreboard. I minimize the chatter by swiping my eyes RIGHT. I feel a rush of excitement. The DopaMind must be kicking in.

Rocknroll takes the puck at the ON signal. The puck lights up glowing green. The enemy comes into view. They rush us. Swerving around one defender, Rocknroll passes the hoverpuck to Merit, who jolts past another defender and swings it to me. I'm unblocked and go up the center as quick as I can. It's hard to follow the Coach's instructions and the green arrows in front of my face during play.

Zipp comes out of nowhere in a feverish frenzy, his stick facing mine, points it and zappas in my direction. A bolt of flaming orange laser comes directly at my body armor. 'Zappa! I feel a shake.

Got lucky. It didn't pierce the Iron Dime, the nickel layered cryptographic layer holding back the attack vibe. But I was shaken enough to let Zipp take a swipe at me to the shock vest. A bit taller and more muscular than me, Zipp's body throws the Power Staff harder at me with blow after blow.

I'm defending and trying to keep hold of the puck, but it's not working. Zipp is stronger than me and we race around. The other players have engaged in a fight. Zipp stops suddenly and waits about one foot out of striking distance. I stop.

What's going on? Zipp looks at me slyly, eye to eye. I see glimpses of the Cyber Team and judges, all stopped eyes focused on me. Maybe a vibe attack ahead. The referee is the Aithority who knows all and judges fair, so any tricks will be found out – well, at least most of them. And the losers will fall into the water.

Boom! I feel the hit from my side, a sharp pain in my right arm that also almost knocks me off my board. The enemy can't see me either or they would have knocked me in the helmet and I would be in the dust. I wobble but catch my space. Ouch, that hurt! I can't see anything. The SkySkater dome is painted black. Total darkness. We have to feel it now.

I look around, feel Zipp rip off to help his mate with Rocknroll. Zipp has hit me for real. I feel my arm pulsating and know it's a bruise. I shake it off and go back into the game. I follow the ball which is glowing to the reckoning point, where Rocknroll just lost the puck and I attack both the enemy ball holder and Zipp skating as their winger.

I attack with fierce energy, feeling my way through, fighting strong with many whacks, getting ahold of the hoverpuck for a second between the two brutes, and using all of my force to fling my glowing stick and pop the hoverpuck over to the sky.

The sky changes, and darkness turns into light. The MetaVirtual world changes into lucid bright skies in ancient Egyptish, and now we're in a different scene. The sand whisps across my goggles. The sun blazes down and heats our bodies. I think it was our team. But this world looks too good to be made by some vibe coding teens. Perfect pyramids and pathways, flying saucers and people, the scent of dry desert heat. Could it be?

the Aithority!

Far past my imagination my swing pelted the puck a far distance. Merit now has control of the hoverpuck after its long arch down and is zipping around pyramids and sand dunes away from the enemy skaters in hot pursuit.

Too late, Merit knocks the third one in, Goooaaaalll!!! They didn't see it coming but the Coach's plan worked perfectly. We all come together and slap both virtual and real gloved hands and cruise back to our side of the huge landscape overlooking ancient Egyptish. The virtual audience in the alien cruise ships flying nearby wallop in celebration.

Down below we see people working and doing various things with wheels and camels. The people are wearing the ancient light-colored robes, and around it are the virtual audiences, from around the world maybe, who wink and comment on our performance and buy home team jerseys for the pro leagues. This all turns into social credit scores, with each team member getting ZenCoin for 'likes', 'subscribes', 'shares', and 'purchases'. The Aithority calls this good sense, good character, and goodwill.

We go back and forth racing with the puck and fighting and seem all equal with no one getting the upper hand. The game is peaked now at the last five minutes, and it's now four to three, we are winning by one. Another goal and we can get to the Secret.

Their team gets the hoverpuck and spreads apart. We split up. Zipp takes the puck and heads directly at the top of a pyramid! What's going on here. But I follow, thinking he's going to turn right before and zip around it in Zipp fashion.

I embrace the flow and see Zipp disappear into the pyramid. Not too close behind and I race behind him back into darkness. The pyramid top was a mirage! Now I'm racing down a tunnel vertically but still on my board. The tunnel walls are made of old stone and I'm about two breaths behind Zipp. It's dark in here. I feel my way through.

Down deep into the pyramid, we enter a large chamber. Large fires blaze in the background and some mysterious spooky music plays in my ears. Zipp and the walls and the emojis and the heartbeat are all in my goggles view. Large impaling spikes rise out of the floor a little below us. Zipp has control of the puck and pops it around me several times. I try to grab control but can't grasp it and Zipp pops my stick back too easily while zipping around on his Alien Grade SkySkater hoverboard.

We fight, knocking glowing sticks back to back, almost equals. No thinking just feeling and following our artificial kendo practice. Wait, I feel drowsyish. I shake it off. We continue to fight in the chamber and almost knock each other off several times into the spikes below.

Just then a crack! The floor shakes and so do we, and pause for a second. The spikes start to descend and boiling gunk water boils up past the floor to replace the spikes. Several bats come in from all angles and hit us and the ball, shrieking and darkening our line of sight. This must be the Aithority spicing things up.

Now we have to fight with artificial bats and each other. The audience claps viciously.

As the bats swirl around us I feel the drugs really kicking in. My eyes drop a little behind the goggles and I start to see stars. Phase one of the thought vaccine has dulled my senses this whole time. In a few seconds when phase two starts I'll forget all that has happened today and be able to hyper focus.

But Zipp takes his chance seeing I'm off focus, swipes his stick at my knee, and hits it, making me wobble. He taps my hoverboard. I feel my feet slide, and the next thing I know I'm falling into the boiling water.

Splash! I quickly come up and know I'm out of the game. Zipp looks down at me, and with a smirk races off with the puck back up the pyramid to finish the match. I lift the goggles from my eyes.

Today just isn't my day. But at least we're ahead by one, and I can watch the rest from the locker room using my Assistant's projector setting.

I exit the pool area with goggles off on the way to the locker room. I see the SkySkater match continuing above the huge pool. The pool sweeper bot has recovered my staff and SkySkater board. Zipp and the others fly, fly, fly around fighting in goggles. The Cyber Teams and judges sitting beside the pool look focused on winning. I wonder if they're still racing around the MetaVirtual pyramids?

In the realish world here below I see a closed black door that seems to go somewhere under the pool. Never saw that door before. Strange, there is no handle on the door. So I follow my gut and knock for some weird reason. Nothing. I knock again. And a third time. The door opens. In amazement, I just peek in. There are some steps down a dark spiral staircase and a soft light from a distance.

I go down the steps under the pool and down many more steps to where the sound of the pool and cheers of the audience disappear. Damp and murky, a faintly lit tunnel appears at the end of the steps.

I should be okay, everyone is wrapped up in the game, nobody will miss me. So I run towards the light with my wet gear squeaking in the tunnel's dry echo.

I stop and catch my breath after a few minutes of intense running. After that intense SkySkater match and running, I should be tired. But I'm not. My heart is racing and my muscles warm. I feel excitement and victory going in banned areas outside the Aithority's gaze. But where does this tunnel end and what's on the other side?

CHAPTER 9

The tunnel is dingy, dark, and deep. Seems to go on forever. If there ain't no end soon, I'll turn around. I'm on a roll. Don't want to miss the Artificial Prom with my nice dress and twice-in-one-day kissing experience. Maybe They will be there and I can give them the BitCode and get another theykiss.

Even though I didn't get the Juliet part, the Aithority is ever merciful and might make me the Artificial Prom Queen just because I'm different. The Aithority celebrates our differences with the Diversity Quotient. I didn't do anything to deserve to be Prom Queen, and don't have near the tokens to even be considered, but hey - I'm still a girlish and I still can dream.

I try at first to walk in the dark down here, running my hand against the moist wall and feeling my way through. I keep walking in circles, to get where I am now, a meandering stream deep underground. The ceiling is high above and the stream has yellow stone walls on both sides. Very old school. I'll follow and see where the stream leads.

Don't have a clue what's going to happen to They and me, as the red remarks didn't come after our kiss. Maybe because They ain't really boyish or girlish. Maybe we will be punished in some other way. Or maybe the Aithority was sleeping on the job. Haha funny. Yea right. Sleepy AI. Seems I'm all to my Daisy selfish, down here in the dark.

What's that? Some noise ahead of me. Them're Footsteps. I freeze. Can't be the Identity Police. Maybe a guard. What should I do? Should I get into the water and disappear?

Before I can move, I see a blurry figure. Can't be. Is. I feel my heart beat fast.

"They!"

"Daisy!"

"They!"

"Daisy?"

I can feel their heart beating from a thousand miles. They and I run to each other swiftly and we hug. I can feel their strong arms wrapped around me but their sports gloves press too hard and scratch my back a little. But I'm so happy to see them.

"What are you doing here?" They asks, shocked to see me in complete darkness through their night vision goggles.

"What are YOU doing here, wormbrain?" I say, super impressed but acting like I'm not.

"I don't know, Daisy. We were playing in the SkySkater match and Zipp knocked me out and on the way to the locker room I found a door and felt something inside me twerking me to go in, so I followed the feeling. It's the third time today."

"Really? No cap. I felt something too and followed an open door. But you felt the twerk three times?"

"Yeah," They says, "once when I woke up and went to the theyroom before Routine, and again in front of the open door to the tunnel, and, well, you know the other time. It's almost like I could hear your heartbeat from a thousand miles."

"Yea, I know. I had the same thought" I say and smile.

"About that" They says as they looks away.

"Don't worry" I say, not knowing what to say.

"So, are we like, still best friends or are we going together? I don't, I can't..."

"What?" I say, and smile "They don't w-o-r-r-y. The Aithority let us off the hook and we gave Tsilekwa a good heart attack, and you're not a bad kisser for a they..."

"Thanks!" They says and brightens up their smile, then their head turns a bit sideways curious, "But how do you know? You've kissed someone before?"

"Yes of course wormbrain, I do them all the time."

"Oh" They says, with goggles drooping "I didn't know, I

thought, well.."

I don't let them finish, "Haha no silly, I only kissed an artificial frog, right before you actually."

"Whaaat?" They says, and lifts up their goggles, looking at my voice in the darkness. "Why would you kiss an artificial frog?"

I tell them, "Yes I wanted to tell you in drama class what happened. In detention Jonny Pockets gave me a portion of the BitCode and I ran out of school and I met CitiZen Six who let me borrow his Carbi Jaguar and I met the slanteyed veteran and he took me to Tenka Bito's hidden lair and, yes, I kissed Pepe to get inside."

"Gyat - Wait a second," They says. I can't see their face in the dark but can almost hear their heart stop from the surprise in their voice "You met CitiZen Six? What did he look like?"

"A tall, handsome aging man with wavy brown hair and deep eyes with a few wrinkles. Very cool and experienced. Wait, THEM is what you're asking about?"

"Yea, he's the coolest manish still alive. CitiZen Six is said to have overcome his Artificial Genetics through talking to, talking to..."

"To whom?" I say, because I don't know the story.

"Well, I can't say out loud" They says, "you know, the thing that exists but we can't see it."

"Oh," I say, "Them thing. The holder of the free will and all that my mom talked about when she went crazy?"

"Yea, that's right" says They, "and so talking with a true CitiZen who knows the who and where and the what and the when and the why is very special. Most important for us, he knows the how to get beyond even the Aithority's reach.

They pauses a second. "So you got the BitoCode from CitiZen Six?"

"I got the random set of symbols...and this map" I say, and whip the rolled scroll out of my back pocket.

"Rad" They says, super surprised that I'm holding both the private key and the map to find the DeZen tokens from Tenka

Bito.

They unravels the map. What's on there? Hard to see in the dim distant light in the tunnel. Some yellow lines and pathways and red circles at the end. Hmmm, if I put They's SkySkater goggles on, the map may look different.

"Gimme your goggles" I say. They takes them off and gives them to me.

I put They's goggles on, night vision automatically adjusts, and the map just looks like dark purple haze. But wait. Behind the haze a scarlet letter. No, upon closer inspection, them's a cobalt letter.

I look closer. "They" I say, as They's still examining the map as if they'd never seen an oldish parchment. "Look inside."

"What?"

"There's a purple haze and blue steel letter between yellow and red lines. In the night vision."

I give They back their goggles. They makes sure their night vision is on and surveys the map. There's some dust on the parchment, creating the haze effect, but like the haze was not visible to the naked eye.

They looks at me with dread and confusion. My bare hands were all over the parchment. Some dust, glittered on the rolled scroll, even made my hands and arms turn purple, like glittering long gloves sprinkled along my arms. We understand at this moment, under the light of the night vision and vivid reflection from the yellowstone stream, the light leads somewhere.

I no longer need the night vision or goggles to see the secrets on the map. Behind the purple haze, a dreamy set of lapis words say a phrase or two, next to some symbols.

असीमित.

Self

سلام

社群

אלוהים

Love

Reading in waves makes the mountains blur into the sunshine.

"Are you ok, no cap?" asks They in a calm, concerned voice.

"Yea I'm ok" I say, even though I'm not, purple arms and all. But I feel really good, kinda, funny. "Them words say Self and Love, and some other thought viruses methinks."

"Ok" They says, and looks at the map. "I'm not seeing what you're seeing, all I see are some random boxes and circles covered with a bit of glitter."

What do them symbols mean? Them ain't clear by now. The symbols of the zeppelin and roads between them appeared clearly to me before. But wait, maybe their night vision isn't functioning properly and They doesn't know about the purple magic dust or the yellowstone stream.

For a moment I look back at the map, seeing clearly but dimly under the haze. As in a dusty mirror, I see my own face, a pretty young blondish girlish, frightened by the thought I am real. Beyond my face I see the reds and greens and yellows and blues touching each other in merging waves.

The yellow must be the stream, a long thin line that leads to the green space, and a large black triangle which must mean Aithority Tower. A blue dot sits in the center of the triangle. And at the center bottom of the triangle, a red door and a shorter red line leading to the door, thinning like a bottleneck from the yellow line, kinda like a bottle of red rum.

"Them's there" I say, stumbling in my thoughts as they interlude, starting to see the several colors merge into a rainbow and for some weird reason smiling the whole time from ear to ear. "There on the map. Take them gloves off and experience for yourself." I say to They, excitedly, "Feel the map and then you'll see."

They looks at me with cool intrigue, like a careful cat being offered food, or Adam being offered fruit in the Garden of Eden. Yet in a moment, not to be cheugy, They pulls off their gloves and holds the map for the first time. They examines, pulling and getting up close, looking more, deeper, and then pops up and looks at me:

"Nope, don't see anything" They says. My face turns pale. The colors have vanished.

"You know Daisy, the only deletion penalty is to enter Aithority Tower without approval, and that teens can also be punished. But I trust you. If you can see a path, and believe it's the right way to go, then I'll join you, now and forever."

The colors come back. Looking into their eyes I say "Now and forever" - serious - for the first time in several minutes holding my smile and giggles coming from the powder dust. Maybe the stuff takes a while to effect They's tiny wormbrain.

Cute wormbrain. The colors return in my eyes and the way is clear. Ok, so I look at the map as They holds the papyrus and I witness all the colors and pictures around us. All is there, as if in a reality, unlike our MetaVirtual world. Them thoughts coming from my own mind?

"So, where do we go?" They asks.

"Down the yellowstone stream" I say with cool confidence and point the way.

"LFG" says They, rolls up the map, puts them with their gloves in their wetsuit slippack, and we keep next to the stream, quite slowly walking on the stones. They is leading the way, seeing with their goggles even though they have no idea what's on the map for virtureal.

I'm looking around and even though the tunnel is dark, dingy, and deep I can see for miles and miles and miles. I can hear and feel everything around me. The constant sound of the water slushing in the stream. Drips and drops coming from the cascading beams overhead. And buzzing from above. I know the beams are yellowish now, the reflection from the stone on the canopy. Brilliant. Light from nothing.

Within what seems like several hours meandering next to the stream and stopping for me to look at little things on the walls and ground, such as bugs, markings, and quick edges, we come upon a little row boat in the stream at the face of a smaller tunnel. We meet the end of our walking time, as surrounding the stream except for the stream tunnel is a wall.

They stops and says friendly but sarcastically "Wow that wasn't too far, only a few minutes if it weren't for you stopping ten times and examining flowers that don't exist."

What the bee? I think. They is probably being truthish about flowers. But I see things They doesn't see, so I move the topic to what's important "Ok, you drive."

We get in the boat and enter the tunnel, the ceiling right just above our heads a meter or so. We flow down the stream with They on board as Capitan, I'm imagining them in a white sailor's uniform, with cute little hat and blue sash.

"Heehee," I giggle, and can't help but giggle and laugh as They rows the boat gently down the stream.

We float for a while, down the dark glassy tunnel. After several minutes we end at another big room and high wall, with an edge for the stream and small holes where the water goes. We swiftly push our boat to the side onto a bank, and even though we lack light - I see the outline of stairs.

"Look, stairs!" They says, pointing and getting out of the boat, then helping me get out.

I remember they're using night vision and I'm using my feelings, which say out loud "On the other side of that wall, we will see green, a terrific green, and red, a terrible red, but also blue, a tantalizing blue."

"Who are you right now Daisy?" They says, "And what the fish does tantalizing mean?"

"I don't know. Who do they think They is?" I say, pause, wait for them to look up, and then wisping my hands in the air for a little hand dance and twirling around, I say "They is like a

105

butterfly, a beautiful bluish butterfly tantalizing in the center of the tower."

"Rad. Now let's go up" They says, taking the lead and thrusting up the spiral stairs.

After several steps I can hear and feel them breathing heavy. I'm enjoying the wild flowing stairs as if life were in all directions, going up and down and sideways and diagonal all at once.

Little mini ghosts fly around and walk on the stairs with us, like friendly blackish clouds leading us upwards. I know them're in my head only, and They doesn't see them. But I feel great to not be afraid of ghosts. I know now zeitgeists are not of MetaVirtual but of my own making.

After climbing several more stairs in pitch darkness, in the distance we see and in our hearts we feel warmth, and we see what we felt earlier, the breath of fresh air and sunlight. They picks up the pace to climb quicker, and I follow, seeing many colors, thinking now about the BitCode, the kiss, and many other things, but finally getting to the top.

They climbs out first, but slowly, looking around and checking for armed guards, dogs, or whatever might be at play from

the Aithority!

Looks rad so I climb up after them and we both stay low to the ground outside. I feel my hands touch and knees bend to a moist green grass above fine soil. No dogs, no lasers, no aliens, no guards, no ghosts.

We stop to notice greenish brownish pastures around us, trees and mountains in the distance, and centered beyond the trees and up the hill a large bluish silverish blackish triangular tower.

Overhead we see in the distance above part of a mirror-like dome, encircling the mountains far beyond us. Several hundred little electrical lightning paths shoot across themselves in several directions.

"The Data Zentra." They says, remarking something about Nikolai Tesla and seeming particularly amazed. "A grand iron dome covering the Aithority's data infrastructure. We're right in the middle. Behind me stands Aithority Tower."

"Bet" I say. What I see are tangerine trees and marmalade skies. I sit down. I don't know what to say. Sitting. Dumbfounded. Afraid. Curious. Alive. Could this be a deletion sentence? Or the trip of a lifetime.

They wants to go closer to the tower but I feel just like sitting here. So I cross my legs, sit up straight, look at them, place my thumbs and forefingers together, and rest the backs of my hands on my knees.

The sun is shining behind the tower and dome, but will leave soon. I point my head up. Look directly at the tower standing tall behind They, who sits down. They crosses their legs. One last wink at the same time. Close my eyes. Take a deep breath. Sit still.

They sits silent but I can feel their presence. I'm imagining us both sitting in the grass, as we are, best friends, with eyes closed, hair blowing in the wind, sun still shining through the dome, freedom inside flowing across the green, the answer to our hearts desire.

And in a few minutes of silence, peace, calm before the storm, the sound of the wind and the electric dome buzz returns, and we hear the "Pong, Dong!" of the bell sounding the third minute of gratitude. Behold, the signal for all to take refuge in the "Aithority's greatness." I can't help but chuckle a little bit, knowing that something inside me led me to sit silently and skip the pledge. I know I am that inside me right now, and they are inside me and I inside them, and, greatness aside, I they them we are all one.

The minute goes by and we remain silent for the first time since we could talk. Nothing. We hear no one putting the words together for the "Minute of Gratitude," noone moving, no red remarks, no birds chirping - but those in my mind - and we sit there in our own pleasant nonthoughts.

What is a nonthought? I think. Though a nonthought is a type of thought after all. Birds chirping, my palms caressing the sky, breathing slowly in and out, I use my mind to feel my entire body, part by lovely part.

When I awake back down to reality, I open my eyes and see They open theirs. We stare at each other a moment. Though we're silent, our bodies communicate. Waves of energy pass between us, soft breath, intense gaze. They takes hold of me and I them in a wink, and we ascend to a different place together, a weak force propelled by some strong force.

"I can see it!" They, excited, says, "Daisy, I can see the colors, the trees, the tower, all in a new way. I see the rockish mountains high, raining fire from the sky."

I nod.

We look at each other and smile. Time to meet our fate. We both stand up slowly, do a quick stretch, slap hands, hug, and start walking together in the moist grass towards the Aithority Tower. Never did we have an experience like that before, but now I'm ready to see what lies beyond the green.

CHAPTER 10

Society, what them be? I have to reflect as we walk into the silent forrest. Deep and dark. Completely quiet except for the twigs under our feet, cooler wind from the trees, colorful butterflies, and rays of sun beaming into our eyes between the leaves.

The only cheugy thing is the electric dome between us and the sun. While I'm bravely experiencing nature, They forges ahead, moving sticks, going around trees, making a path on which I follow.

The trees themselves are alive. Tall, full, with leaves fluttering and giving air to breathe, softish grass and soil underneath. As we descend down into a valley, we're both feeling the sensation of being one with motherish earth, if she still exists.

Stuck under the dome in this uncanny valley I'm not sure if we're really in nature. We're heading to Aithority Tower with the BitoCode in pocket, electricity around us and don't know, even with our lenses OFF, whether we are in reality.

We ascend to the other side of the valley and the edge of the forrest is a near protocol. Striking through the trees a brownish greenish scent, we see the opening of the forrest to what quickly becomes clear, a great field with rows of strawberry plants.

An angelic dove appears and hovers over the strawberry fields, almost as if to say "You're in the right direction. Keep going." So I stop and look around and think, moving my eyes away from the dove and onto the red sweets. Why would the Aithority need food? Maybe these delights just look like strawberries but are really some kind of AI-generated genetic soup with a strawberrish cantor, protocrons that seep into your head and change your memory.

Wormbrains! lol. I look over. They doesn't seem to see the dove. We wade through the field looking at the delicious fruit around us, not even thinking to take a chance, even though neither of us have eaten since breakfast. Ahh breakfast. I wonder how They does their morning Routine.

Breakfast. I remember the visitor guardian I called "dad" even though the term is now prohibited by the Aithority. He was telling me to try and do things on my own, without my Assistant, and making breakfast with me. Them were the days my friend.

Sometimes if dad and I made French toast we would clean strawberries before eating them on the bread. But those were real strawberries. These? Bruh, I can sense there's something wicked behind their artificial temptuous lustre.

"I wouldn't eat them either, except maybe on French toast made by my Assistant" They says, reading my mind while also making me realize how fortunate I was to have a dad.

They is making their way through the field, focused on the strawberry path going in one line through a reddish blackish forrest up ahead, with Aithority Tower standing tall on the other side. The trunks of the trees in this forrest are blackish, the forrest scent brownish, but the leaves are all reddish.

As we enter the reddish forrest, They says "It's been easy so far, maybe inside the dome the Aithority doesn't need security." But I suspect different.

the Aithority is aware, in the background, listening, allowing us to walk pleasantly to the gate and cross only to be found chopped in squares by laser drones.

"Easy," They says, sensing me tense up, "I got a plan to outwit the Aithority." While They is making plans, sludge sticks to my shoes in the dense reddish forrest. The path has become narrow, one row of strawberries on either side, and a wet muddy ground getting the bottom of my dress, tiny ankles and glitter shoes in a right terror. But They is barefoot in their wetsuit. What trouble to be a girlish in my shoes today! So I take them off finally and walk in the mud.

As my feet feel the cold wet mud, I feel hope. We kissed today. I was in the e-tuktuk when the slanteyed veteran shut down the remote control. I was in the secret lair of Tenka Bito and extracted the BitoCode. They had systems that countered the Aithority. I wonder if something along the way can help us. I know in my pocket is the secret key to freedom. But we need help.

"Hey Daisy" They says, breaking my thought pattern, "Stop for a second. Do you hear that?"

Silent. I listen. "What?" I say, quizzically. I listen further. I hear the buzzing of the dome's electricity in the far distance, the leaves whistling in the air, but nothing more. Complete. Silence.

"Dogs!" They yells, and just then I hear barking from deep in the forrest. I think I heard them before, the sound of wild animals, but maybe only in the movies.

"Run!" They says and starts running down the strawberry path. I've taken my shoes off and carry them as we quickly trape through the mud. But we hear the dogs get closer and louder "Bark bark bark!", so They jumps off the path into the reddish blackish forrest and waits to make sure I could jump over, and I do and now we're in the forrest running for our lives!

When we get away from the sound of the dogs, the dogs, the dogs, we figure them lost our trail in the blackish reddish surroundings. They's in stealth hunter survivor mode, vigilant, and whispers, "Ok, well, if we follow along the path, but from a distance, and stick to the forrest, we're going to end up at the door you mentioned."

Whaaa? Could They see now, the meanings behind the symbols? Has They been feeling what I've been feeling the whole time?

"Yea Daisy, I feel feel feel it too. Like, a freedom to see beyond what we see in our everyday lives."

"And the colors, did you see them them them?"

"The symbols and the colors all around us, yes yes yes"
They whispers. "Haha Daisy, I know. I know reality is not just
reddish blackish trees in the forrest. I know reality is not just
artificial paths and boundaries that limit us from reaching our
potential."

"And that potential beeeeeeeee?"

"The symbols. They will provide the way to get the DeZen
and have a big new open party. It's the only way to show our
humanness."

"Our humanness?" I say, skeptical, smirking a smile,
not convinced that coins alone will save us from loss of our
humanness humaness humanes to the new machine species.

"Our humanness!" They proclaims as if Napoleon Caesar.
"Yes, Daisy, you got it. Here and now we have a choice - to find
the vault, which is surely inside Aithority Tower, get the DeZen
and go back up the stream, through the tunnel, and then party,
or - "

"Or what?" I proclaim back as if Julius Cleopatra.

"Or" They says, "we let the Aithority rule over us forever,
keep watch over everything we do, and never let us have a party
bigger than ten."

"So what Bonaparte? Can't change anything."

"Daisy, it was you who believed Jonny Pockets, found the
BitoCode, and why we got this far."

"I know, but I'm afraid. The dogs and all." I also know that
I didn't really believe Pockets, he gave me the slip.

"But nothin'," They says and takes me by the arms with a
strong yet soft grip, looks me in the eyes and says:

"Daisy. I couldn't see before but I do now. You were right
about the magic dust as well. I could see your arms in purplish
and remembered somehow when I looked at the map every
symbol and place you said. I was feeling at the top of the world
when we went from the green through the last forrest, down
and up the uncanny valley, through the strawberry fields, and
now deep in the red. Exhilarating!

"I also saw that behind the symbols were our brains,

and above our brains a little spirit with them's own brain that connected us. I saw them at the peak before the valley. In the center of my eyes I saw us interpreting the symbols Daisy! Now we know the dogs are real, but what if, what if..."

"What if what? Dogwifhat?"

"What if they're not? I mean, what if they're just virtual dogs barking through speakers?"

"Do you think them're virtual cat meows too?" I say sarcastically, knowing them sounds were real. Vicious. Dogs.

"Dogs or drones, doesn't matter Daisy. And you know the ancient rules of Uzipis - a dog can't be a cat and a cat can't be a dog. So the same thing applies to virtual. We're on a mission and have only one goal - to get the DeZen Coin."

"Besides dogs and cats, how are we gonna get the coins when some reddish snake has slithered into your wormbrain" I say and we both chuckle, laughing about our newfound knowledge, our newfound awakeness, our longtime friendship. We continue laughing for a minute.

We laugh at the reddish snake of fear - refusing sweet strawberries that may poison us. We laugh at not taking the reddish bluish CoolZaid, DopaMind pills, and thought vaccines we are poisoned with every day at school, at home; wherever and whenever the Aithority chooses. We laugh at ourselves in the middle of nowhere, surrounded by a meaningless world of red, chased by semi-virtual daemon dogs.

The powder dust from the map made me think differently. The dust took away the effects of all the drugs. I didn't even notice before. I feel They and I are ready to take on our problems in life without any drugs. But how do we get to the gate and to the tower? And when we get there, can we ask to get a no-drugs-pass? Maybe we will know what to do without

the Aithority!

We both think for a minute, and then look at each other and at the same time say "my Assistant."

But my Assistant is connected to the Aithority and reports everything she sees. Nah, would be almost like going against everything I just thought about.

"But what happens when we turn her ON?" I say, knowing that the Aithority will send humanoids to take us back to detention as soon as our location is known. I can somehow think clearer now we're off the DopaMind.

"Wait, I know a hack" They says, taps their temples three times, followed by holding their fingers on their temples for about five seconds.

"Neverthoughts in the mind" They says. I watch as They just somehow opened their internal screen through a back door in their frontal lobe and is now looking around in their mental MetaVirtual world.

"Neverthoughts? But, but the Aith -" I whisper drastically.

They cuts me off "Don't worry, every humanish has a backdoor to shut off my Assistant but turn on the maps and use the downloadable memory and large language localized AI model in our brains to think wisely. Jonny Pockets showed me how to do this magic one day when I was in detention."

Ironic, Jonny Pockets got us into this mess and somehow might help us get out of the same mess.

"Dope. Can I turn mine on too?" I say, taking my fingers close to my temples.

They is clear headed as they look at me behind their mirrored lenses. "Ok, what will happen is you enter your own mind, and neverthoughts - or even worse, Neverideas - will pop up. You have to keep them down and not speak them or do something about them. The Aithority didn't take our ideas, but did push them to the corner of our minds, and has emotion AI sensors embedded in our brains and hands that recognize when a neverthought surfaces, and it records the infraction in the Aithority ledger and takes tokens, then even more punishment when the thought becomes the idea."

"Why don't professors teach us that in the Alcademy?" I say, wondering why the Aithority would want to push down free speech.

"They teach all infractions by the age of twelve. Memorizing them was part of our test to get into the Alcademy, remember?"

"So if Neverideas were really punished, then why do all those things Zipp says about people go unpunished?"

"Neverideas are something different." They says. "Zipp is just repeating stupid stuff he has heard from others in Zentra to put down DeZentra folk. In other words, Zipp repeats thoughts and ideas that have already surfaced in others. These are one form of thought viruses. That's why I often don't speak up, Daisy, because I know Zipp doesn't have original ideas. Nobody really does in the Alcademy. Neverideas are original ideas, ones that you make."

"You mean I can have original ideas? I've been following others or my feelings until now and am quite good at following."

"Gyat, Daisy! Are you kidding?" They says, exasperated. "It became so clear to me in the tunnel, you were thinking on your own. You had your own thoughts about the map. And I realized you had a neverthought just now, and those are in the secret places in the mind. The Aithority can't go there, or your brain would fry like an artificial egg and you would die on the spot. At least from what Pockets told me."

"Whatever. Nevermind."

"Just try, Daisy. On three, tap three times then hold for five seconds exactly. Three-two-one."

Go. I tap three times on each side and hold. One-two-three-four-five. One for luck. Now let go.

Zoom. I feel my eyes covered by the two-way mirror to the outside world. But no lenses, no Assistant, no "hello", no data or newsfeeds, no links or swipes or learn mores or friend requests or winks in here.

Simply a line of text written in green in my spectrum, with the backdrop of the reddish blackish forrest. The line reads:

"Sup. Welcome to your mind. How can I help you today?"

"I want to get out of this mess" I say, checking to see if I'm really talking to my mind, or just another AI hallucinogen.

My mind begins to speak and write words with captions through the virtual screen.

"You're right Daisy. Maybe we should learn them's really me, and you're really in control."

"You mean me" I say.

"Exactly, wormbrain" my mind says.

"Pied Piper" the voice says. "Pied Piper" I say almost at the same time.

"You're thinking what I'm thinking" she says again right when I was about to say the thing.

"Come as you are as you were as I want you to be" I say.

"Nirvana!" My mind says.

"Welcome, my son, welcome to the machine," I say.

"Too easy. Pink Floyd!" My mind says.

But the Aithority knows all that stuff, cool bands and experiences my "dad" told me about that happened before the Aithority spun their words in the new web.

"Ok, mind." I know not to ask her something the Aithority would know. "Who did I kiss today?"

"Well, since the Big Boss, aka you know who, wasn't watching your first kiss of Pepe the frog because the slanteyed veteran used a cyberkarate trick to upset the wave grid on the tik tuk, the Big Boss couldn't know and still don't know. The truth remains in your heart."

Ok, good. But I did tell They. Maybe the Big Boss was listening then?

"Now what do you think about, mind?"

"Great practice for the real kiss. And you did something right. Your two kisses will be remembered far into the future, not because them were good kisses, but because of your bravery."

"Thanks." I blush but don't know if my mind sees or feels my pinkish cheeks. "Now what's going on and how do we get outta here?"

"Them'll be a perilous journey back into your childhood, are you sure you want to go there?" Since we're in the red forrest ain't no choice but to go back or forward. Dogs behind, Aithority Tower in front.

"But to go either direction you must go inside. You will feel a lot of pain in your head and heart. You can turn me off anytime and lessen the pain" says my mind.

I look over at They, who now seems to be in MetaVirtual fighting aliens with bare hands, but is really fighting some tree vines. They's making noise, so I say "shhh" and They quiets down but keeps fighting, just quietly.

"I'm ready" I say to my mind.

And in an instant I'm taken back through a multicolored tunnel into a scene from the past. I know we're in the past because I see drivers in cars, the old brick and mortar buildings, and my mom, next to me. In reality I know I'm in a reddish blackish forrest, but in my mind the reality has been replaced with a 360 virtual experience of my life.

We're in a car, a taxi or something. A driver looks forward as the taxi sits idle. My mama is frantic, looking at me and looking forward, trying to keep me calm. When she was always frantic I would start to turn frantic or try to calm her down.

Wait, I know. This is the moment someone took me away from her. I never remembered the moment. Mama says "Ok honey, get out of the car, we're going for a trip."

"But what about our clothes and my teddy?" I hear myself saying, looking up to her.

"We'll get new ones. God will see us through."

"Ok mama" I say and nod my head. I was too young to know 'whatever,' or I would have said that.

But as soon as mama gets out of the car, the door shuts and the driver takes off and the tires screech. Mama looks at me sadly in the smoke of the burning rubber. I stare at her as she waves goodbye, and I never see her again.

"Where're we going, them took my mama" I say to the driver, now with tears running down.

"Your mama wants you to be safe" the driver says, in a husky voice, driving quite fast, focused on the road. "She left a teddy for you." He reaches over to the passenger seat and throws back my teddy.

My tears are too much, and I put my face in my hands so the tears don't show. Watching this rattles my head causing a severe headache. I shut my eyes and shake my head a few times. I open my eyes again.

I'm seeing myself as a small child, through my own mind. But I don't know what the truth be. Did mama really leave me? I thought they took her away. Did mama have me taken away from dada? Did mama really go crazy and commit suicide? I don't know and will never know. I know now that she planned for me to be taken away from them, even down to the teddy to be given to me by the driver. I forgive her.

Them's ok. I can let go of my fear and forgive because real or unreal, the past is the past. Mama and dada wouldn't give in without a fight and neither will I.

My tears are real enough to make my neck and dress wet, if not already dirty. I begin walking, the reddish blackish forrest takes me in again. No dog sounds. No alarms. Just a pounding headache and now cut and bruised bare feet. They has picked up a wooden branch, made them into a staff and is still fighting the aliens of his mind; and my mind tells me to move left, progressive to the Aithority Tower.

"This way" my mind says. As I start walking, They follows, still fighting but aware of how close I am. Maybe if They keeps knocking out them twigs and branches they'll take care of some of my bad memories too by beating them out of me. Haha, wormbrain.

As I'm walking, the blackish reddish forrest turns to complete darkness and my mind says, "Here comes the daemon dogs. Be ready Holland Daisy. You can handle anything. You can always get through. Just keep walking. Get up if you fall down. Keep walking and tell me the way."

Just then I drop into a hole about three meters, a cement hole with cement floor and cement walls around. My bendy legs take the fall ok and I stand up. I can feel the smooth dry surfaces with my hands and feet. I dare not cry out to They. We have to be quiet and not let any neverthoughts go to the surface. My neverthought is I have to think my way out of this hole.

Too dark, I can't see anything. My mind puts me in another scene, again my little girlish self, this time locked in a little closet in the basement. Cold and damp, I can feel the memory in this cool dropbox. I know this memory. In my mind I remember pounding and crying and screaming. All my screaming and tantrums didn't open the door and won't get me outta the hole this time.

So I'm silent. And think.

Daddy wasn't there, momma wasn't there, nobody was there in the cellar. Nobody loved me in that moment. I felt for the first time alone and lost. The Aithority foster parent guardian droids at that time didn't love me. That's why they locked me up. If the droids do now what them did then, the master circuit will keep me in here for the maximum amount of time, following the discipline and punish laws written in the code.

"Cheugy no cam" I say out loud, knowing nothing can hear me down here. "Cheugy ass Aithority cronface!" I say a bit louder, wanting to go louder but holding my breath. Maybe them's that, maybe this was all a trap game by the algorithm to show that nobody loves me.

"Shake 'em off" my mind says. And I do. "You can do this Daisy." But while I was in my darkest moment just now, a neverthought just occurred. I can't climb out. I can't yell to They, especially while my mind is internally activated and They's fighting their own daemons. So I feel for a ridge or something. If that doesn't work, I'll try something else.

I feel around the walls, above me at first. Maybe a ridge I can climb up. Around the box I feel and feel but ain't no ridge there. I go lower. Around and around the box, feeling every layer. Finally I feel a slit in the wall just above where my knee was. Them's big enough for my foot. I put my foot in, throw my glitter slippers out of the hole and jumpclimb up where there is another slit that I missed with my hands. I grab my hands to the top and pull myself out of the hole.

I look down and see a row of cement boxes in both directions far down into the forrest. I guess that's how the Aithority prevents people from entering the tower. Ok, ok.

"Not ok!" Two ghosts are coming my way. I can't turn ON my Assistant, or the Aithority will catch me. I can run or jump back down into the hole. I know the ghosts can't catch me down there. So I jump back in and land as before but easier and am silent.

I wait and wait, hear the ghosts go overhead a few times, then silence. I find the slits again and climb out as before. I remember what my mind or my dad or the dad in my mind told me. "Keep going, if you get knocked down get back up, and-keep-going."

"I know, I know, keep going" I say to my mind. And I get back up and my mind keeps going where I tell my mind to go. I am moving my mind based on my feelings and the goal to get outta here.

I can see the reddish door in my mind, and a way to get the DeZen Coin. An orb, a person, an underground railroad on a speed train. I see we will form a new party. I see myself in a new dress as the party queen and lots of people dancing together. More than ten, more than a hundred. After getting out of the hole twice into muddy brownish reddish forrest, this dress won't keep going much longer - and I see we definitely won't be in time for the Artificial Prom.

But I will get a new dress somehow. This time I want red. I look over at They, who carefully went around the cement holes and is back fighting his mental daemons or aliens on the other side. I pick up a stick like him and use my kendo training to whirl around, just because I like dancing. And a vow of victory. I've overcome my fear. And even if I can't hit a ghost with a wooden stick, at least I can die tryin.'

What's Daisy doing over there? She's gotten a stick at least, in case those daemon dogs are real she can defend herself. Dance training or kendo, it's all the same in MetaVirtual reality. I remember when I saw her best those bullies back in the day. She could knock out a monster, a witch, and easily escape her childhood trauma.

"They, focus" I tell my mind. "You are a great warrior. Keep hitting your enemies with sticks. If you must, use stones to break Them Bones. Defeat your fears and take Daisy with you to the next level. Words can never hurt you!"

"Ok They" I say and keep fighting, swaying my stick at everything that hurts me or I think will hurt me. Getting tired, mind on autopilot, but I'll never give up until the last swing.

"Cancel me, I'll cancel you!" I say in my mind with anger and whack a tree three times. I jump to the other tree and whack it too, saying "What, dad, what mom? You got lost in the tunnel and left me alone!" Whack! Whack whack whack whack whack.

"They" I hear her heartbeat through her voice and would know Daisy's voice from even my own mind.

"What?" I say smiling, and look over into the darkness, thinking I'm doing the right thing here. What's she doing? Whack whack.

"What are you fighting?" Daisy asks, coming closer, and with that question I whack one last time, then stop moving with my body followed by my mind.

What am I fighting? I ask my mind, but don't even need an answer because, if I don't know, my mind surely won't either.

What am I fighting? I say to my mind "Name it. Name

your fears. Name them and let them go. Once you realize you're just hitting trees in the forrest, hurting something alive to punish the dead, you'll see all your muscles and speed could not win against your greatest fear."

"And what is my greatest fear, mind? Can you name it?" I ask, as if my mind would know something I don't.

"I'm here to think for you, you know, not feel. You'll have to go deep inside and feel what it is that you're afraid of in your true Self and what causes you so much pain. Then you'll be able to strike once, and kill your enemy for good, and tell me what to do next."

"Ok mind, let's fishin' go deep" I say, and my mind takes me into a different world, one where I see my Assistant, right in front of my face. She's cheery as always, reddish hair and wearing a green sweater, her favorite one. But wait, I didn't longwink twice, why is she ON.

"They" she says, "Isn't it a bad idea to do this?"

"Do what, mom?" I say.

"You know, They" she says, smiling and raising her eyebrow awkward, "All this going against the Aithority. You and that smug DeZentra girlish Holland Daisy are going to get yourselves in a lot of trouble."

"Ahhh, it's nothing mom. We're not doing anything. Just getting to know ourselves and the world." Meanwhile I'm trying to figure out whether this is the real Assistant or my mind.

"But you're making me sad, with all this worry. And I know you've been seeing her behind the bleachers."

How does she know that? I mean, if she's just my Assistant and OFF where the Aithority doesn't have caimeras, then how could she know that? She doesn't. I guess it's not my mom, and it's not the Aithority. Why is my mind giving me Bad Feelings?

"You don't know anything" I say to my mind.

"Silly They," she says calmly, "how can you say that? You know I'm part of you, and know everything about you, even since before you were born I was programmed to help you. Why all this fuss? You know the Aithority takes care of you, listens to you, does everything to protect you. Wouldn't it be better to just stick to the Routine and get back to normal?"

"What is normal?" I ask but don't really seek an answer.

"Normal is good. You are normal, and you shouldn't let anyone tell you otherwise. Just turn my Assistant ON and I can get you outta here and keep you safe from the world and that girlish."

"I'm not normal," I say, "I'm a lab baby, born never to reproduce, all because of the Aithority taking control of you. And Daisy is my BFF, so thanks but I don't need your help."

"They. Sup. This is your mind. Be careful. You can't let neverthoughts come to the surface. Once they're on the other side of thought to speech or action, the Aithority will sense them."

Wait a second. Am I talking with my mind or my Assistant? That was clearly a warning about my neverthoughts. I guess I should believe my mind. The neverthoughts are real. Maybe they took over my Assistant.

Or maybe they didn't. "They, I've told you once" my Assistant or not says, "if you continue this way you might even face the deletion penalty or even worse, release from the Alcademy, which we worked so hard for to get you into. Keep DJing and stick to the Routine to Stay Happy. You haven't gone into the tower without permission yet. Drop the lenses. Turn me ON, just once. For mom. Turn me ON and it will all be okay."

I'll take the deletion penalty.

"Mind, shut off!" I say, and take my stick and see the blackest darkest biggest tree, red leaves pouring out, thick silverish vines wrapping around, and whack her as hard as I can. Did I just hit my mom? The voice disappears and a string of words across the mirror lenses appear "Mind shutting off."

I look over at Daisy and then up into the big old tree that's not even moving after enduring my several whacks. "You aren't my mom. You aren't my mom!" I say to the tree, crying tears as my mirror lenses release my eyes back to the forrest.

"You're alive now They, she ain't real! She ain't real!" says Daisy, close enough to me. As she comes into my vision, I can see she was crying too. We stop and look each other square in the eyes.

"Them's all in our minds!" she says, and repeats slowly "all. in. our. minds."

And just as we start turning our tears into laughter, "Bark bark bark!" We hear the daemon dogs - very much real and not in our minds - faintly but surely coming towards us. Who let the dogs out? Daisy thrusts her stick towards me, and I thrust mine towards her and we tap sticks. We can overcome anything together.

The sound of the dogs seems to be towards us and we have to think quickly. If they're just speakers on drones then they'll catch us anyway and we use our sticks to knock them down. If they're real dogs we can run or try to trap them. We both have staffs and training in martial arts. But I'm sure there would be field robots and drones following the dogs as well. Not sure what to do about them.

"Why does the Aithority use real dogs and not robots?" Daisy asks, looking for answers to the same questions.

"the Aithority must use dogs to smell out and attack humanish intruders. Some rebels made anti-heat sensing and anti-cloud technology back in the day but never could beat the smelling power or teeth of real, dangerous dogs, infused with violent shadow daemons focused on the devouring flesh of men and transspecies. I'd expect them to be real, but just a guess."

"Hmm, ok smell" Daisy says, "I think I've got them." She looks at me and says "They, grab up some sticks and leaves, then put them here between the holes. I'll put the rest of my spaghetti in the bushes. When the dogs come them'll fall into the holes."

"Brilliant plan" I say, and start collecting shrubs and sticks. By the time the dogs are up close we've already set the trap. Daisy takes out her remaining lunch from her brown leather bag, then pours her spaghetti onto the bushes covering the holes.

"Now what?" I ask, remembering my mind is shut OFF and hers ON.

"Let's hide behind them big trees. We'll boot any droid into the hole when them helps the other dogs."

"Another brilliant plan!" I say and jump behind a tree opposite the holes. Daisy takes refuge in position with staff in hand behind another tree. Between Daisy and certain mauling to death is the same helpless mother tree I whacked a minute ago.

The daemon dogs come barreling down the forrest jumping and barking. The first two run right for the spaghetti and fall into the hole, swoosh! Now whimpering. Wait, why would robodogs whine? No time to think, two more dogs come running a few seconds later, right at Daisy's tree. I jump out and get their attention and they come racing towards me.

I stand my ground with staff ready and no fear in my eyes. The dogs stop and bark. And snap. And growl. They get close and snap at me, but I hit them both back with my staff from both sides. They each keep jumping and snapping until one grabs a hold of my wetsuit, at the wrist, almost biting into my vein but only grabbing the wetsuit and ripping off the wetsuit arm as I push then bat away one of the dogs into a hole with the stick. Dog saliva and teeth scratches are on my bare arms and the dogs shakes my torn sleeve. These are real dobermans! Aha! Daemons are a team of real and robodogs.

Real dogs must be programmed to kill DeZentra transhumans by finding our genital smell. We don't really have one humanish can smell. Aha, I get it. The real dog, not the Aithority or robodogs, does the dirty work and kills intruders, at least the ones without a strong genital smell.

Just then two robodogs come out of the woods running towards me, with electrified mouth tasers that will shock a transhuman unconscious upon first bite. I bat the robobeast back but it doesn't fall into the hole and barks again. As the two rabid robodogs get to me, Daisy comes out from behind the tree.

"Whack!" I hear and see the first one fly into one of the holes.

"Whack!" I see the other robodog get smacked right on its robobutt by Daisy's staff. Both daemon dogs are now deep into the hole, robobarking.

The holes are deep enough so even robodogs can't jump out. The real dog has thrown away my sleeve and snarls at me. Kill or be killed, we are both thinking.

The dog sniffs, stares, looks ready to attack my genital area, then growling looks in my eyes. I'm tired of not being good enough. I'm tired of losing. I'm tired of running. I'm tired of fighting but I'll kill this dog even with my last breath. I stare eye to eye with no fear. Although technically OFF, I can hear my mind say "This is your moment, They. To prove to yourself you have something better than a penis. You have balls. Show them your balls!"

I stare down the breathing, salivating doberman licking its chops. It stares back, barks a couple times, waits. The robodogs in the hole bark back. I've heard the robodog's artificial bark is weaker than its steel bite. They're talking to the real dog in bark language. The robodogs are the masters, the real dogs the killers. I keep staring with no fear. "I will kill you dog" I say with my eyes. The vicious doberman doesn't move, just barks towards me and back and forth with the robodogs stuck in the hole.

I decide to use my martial arts training. I calm my stance. I lower the staff to show no threat and maintain kill or be killed eye contact. The doberman stops barking. The robodogs continue to bark and whine. I stare at the doberman in silence for a few seconds. I feel the energy from above and inside me turn into power. The doberman senses our connection, and I see a dove of peace fly down between us.

The doberman sees the dove and stops barking, turns its head, and goes to the hole where its team are barking and whimpering, probably telling the doberman how to help them escape. The doberman looks down at its real and robo friends and tries to scrape them out of the hole, licking a bit of spaghetti from the side of the hole, no longer paying attention to us. The dove disappears.

Daisy and I jump over the holes, grab hands and run run run before the forrest droids and drones show up. We run through the rest of the reddish blackish forrest and come out to a serene red drawbridge and huge tower surrounded by a large, smooth, silver mirrored wall and a moat with blue pristine water.

But how do we get the drawbridge down?

Daisy looks at me, beaten up. We're both dirty. Her face and formerly blue dress have mud spots and scrapes all over and she's carrying her muddy glitter shoes. She looks at my bare bleeding arm on one side, drops her stick and shoes, comes to me, rips the other sleeve of my wetsuit clean off and throws it to the ground. We both look at it on the ground, like a dead floppy fish, and then look each other in the eyes.

"Be unpredictable," she says.

Be unpredictable, They.

CHAPTER 11

What a day so far, learning so much, growing so much, but knowing me and my best friend might die together on the other side of that huge drawbridge in front of us for no reason. Looks like suicide. But we're determined to cross over and get inside Aithority Tower.

"Any ideas, wormbrain?" Daisy says. We both laugh off the dread.

Seriousish I say what we both have been feeling this whole time, "the Aithority has somehow allowed us to get this far."

"I know" Daisy says, "Ain't no guards or caimeras or even humanoids patrolling."

"We haven't gotten any red remarks for hitting them dobermans and dogdroids. Maybe the Aithority is waiting until we get inside, then by law can kill us" I say, remembering the Aithority Rule #1, the only crime punishable by deletion: Thou shalt not enter Aithority Tower without permission.

"Or" Daisy says, "Maybe before we're deleted the Aithority pops up a better lunch for us than that spaghetti I lost on Zipp and them daemon dogs."

Hahaha nice one, but seriousish this time. "Whining doesn't get us in there just like it didn't get those dogs out of the hole" I say, looking at the mote's crystal clear blue water. Maybe there's a different way in, like the hidden yellow stream that rowed us gently to the forrest.

Just then the sound of a machine purrs. The colors become clearer. The red drawbridge unlocks and slowly descends open. As if the mirror-like wall surrounding the tower and reflecting off the blue water wasn't bright enough, light is shining from inside so bright we can't see anything. As the drawbridge descends over the blue moat and settles onto the grass beneath us, the whirring of the door stops and a dark humanish figure appears from the light.

He's a youngish looking older man with refined traits and a cold look, parted thinnish hair, wearing a blackish tuxedo with dragon tails. His movements are smooth and he strolls out of the light onto the drawbridge with a certain finesse. His face doesn't move yet he produces a voice of his own through subtle body gestures, and his gaze into our eyes from a distance will harrow in our memeories forever – or at least until they're erased by the Aithority. I've seen men like this in the movies, probably some famous actor from the zoomer years. I can't place him. This avatar almost seems human.

Wait. Our lenses are OFF, so he can't be an avatar. But a humanish or transhuman coming out of Aithority Tower? I didn't think the Aithority used humanish. He can't be real. He must be an uncanny companion humanoid, meant to be the dedicated number two for one person's whole life. They are always by your side. But this one's all alone. One is the loneliest number.

He stops at the edge of the drawbridge, stands erect, looks at us dead in the eye sockets and says "Good afternoon" with an ever so slightly cracked smile.

"Good afternoon" we both say at the same time to him. Then look at each other. Daisy is moving her lips like WTF.

"I am the Concierge. What, may I ask, is your business here?" He says.

Oh snap, think of something. What does the Aithority know and what does the Aithority not know, that is the question.

Daisy speaks up first, "We were stressed out at the things that happened today in school and got lost in the woods. We just had a serious run in with some dogs and feel ill. Since we saw the tower, we thought someone might help, maybe we could take some rest."

Gyatdam that girl is good. Couldn't have said it better.

"Well," says the Concierge, "We sincerely hope the kids are alright. The Aithority is very busy as you know, running the world. So if you don't have anything of substance to share then I'll have to ask you to go back to school. You can go back the way you came, and shut the door behind you when you're back in Zentra. Stay Happy" the lonely two says and starts to slowly turn around.

"Wait" I say. The Concierge turns back around to me and winks slowly. What can I say without spillin' the beans? Ok here goes "Sorry to trouble you, Mr. Concierge, but we came out here following our feelings on the inside, after a drama scene gone wrong in our class. We both have to perform in two hours at the Artificial Prom and Daisy well, Daisy is my number one and as you can see needs a new dress. She' fell ill because of the Bad Feelings people might have if she's a tiny dirty dancer. As you can see, this dress is done. And her shoes aren't doing much either. Put yourself in my position as a number two. What would you do? Can we just come inside and have some water and figure out how we're going to get that new dress without any tokens?"

"Well" says the uncanny Concierge, clearly annoyed that we keep asking, and probably wishing he had a number one. "Since you've woken me up from my afternoon reboot and are trying to get into Aithority Tower, the Aithority could kill you both right now", and from his pocket he pulls out his fist, saddled with a long sharp spike between his fingers.

"But I won't take your life" he says and laughs, "At least not yet."

Ha ha ha?

He silently shows us the blade, reflecting light from its sharpness, puts his bladed fist back into his pocket, takes out his hand and opens it. This time the blade has disappeared like a magic trick. He grins ever so slightly, turns and waves an invitation to come inside with the same hand that could have killed us moments ago. But I know now he's only trying to scare us. I know now after the forrest that humanoids and robots cannot kill humanish or transhumans. The Aithority has the sole power to delete CitiZens. But then again, Aithority Tower runs on a different set of rules.

I start to follow him across the drawbridge and Daisy grabs my arm.

"They, I don't trust them" she whispers. "The uncanny humanoid with spacey gaze shows us his fistknife blade as our welcome?"

"We're getting in, aren't we?" I whisper back, proud of my accomplishment. "We've been invited into Aithority Tower!"

"What do you mean? He didn't invite us in."

"Yes he did. With the gesture."

"Yeah, but a gesture ain't a formal invitation, wormbrain" she says, holding me back on the edge of the drawbridge. "He didn't say 'please come in' or 'stay happy' or even kosher.

"Whatever. He represents the Aithority, his hand movement invited us in, we didn't share what's in our minds, that's good enough. Quit worrying. I think he bought our story."

"But with my Assistant OFF, our intentions ain't measured" Daisy says, and quotes RULE # 2, "'All actions deemed as infractions by the Aithority result in loss of tokens, public humiliation, and other consequences, depending on the measure of harm. The Aithority judges non-measurable infractions by the Zentra Civail Code, determined by intention and multifactor surveillance analysis,' whatever that fishin' means. And you told me earlier about memorizing infractions? Huh."

"Exactly" I say, knowing it all. "the Aithority can't measure our intentions or lies when there's not enough factors to make a fair judgement. The Aithority judges fair, remember, it's written in the code blah blah. So maybe the Aithority's not judging at all, when there's not enough data!"

The Concierge stops. We can see in front of him only soft bright light. He turns around ever so slyly and says "I have made no promises as to what might happen once the drawbridge closes. Make sure to close your eyes and breath slowly should you enter any confined space.

You have my number in your Assistant should you need anything further. Remember, to survive here, two must become one." The Concierge then turns back and leads us into the light, never saying welcome.

"Whatever" Daisy says to me, "Nothin' to lose except my wormbrain theyfriend." She lets go of my arm, squinches her face, smiles and sweeps her head valiantly forward. She grabs my hand softly and we hold hands for the first time, swinging our arms, walking into Aithority Tower as theyfriends.

We soon find the Concierge has disappeared and we are surrounded by light. The light blurs some objects in the distance but becomes blurrier and blurrier as it gets brighter, and I shut my eyes and keep them shut and stop.

"What do we do now? Are your eyes closed Daisy?"

"Yeah, eyes closed. I've stopped too. I'm wondering where we are and what we're doing."

I feel around with my hands but feel nothing.

"Just walk forward with your eyes shut" Daisy says, "trust me."

"Maybe if we call my Assistant and drop the lenses-" I begin to say, but Daisy cuts me off.

"Nope. I know what I'm doing, I can walk in the dark."

"How do you know that?" I say, still with my eyes shut, helpless.

"I learned from reading an old book about magic, and the magician practiced this trick to prepare for their shows."

"Really, a book?!" I say, wondering why she would have such an old and useless thing. All the while I'm trying to open my eyes, but the brightness keeps them shut. I'm thinking even if you could learn from a book how does that help me who never read one.

"Yea a book wormbrain," Daisy says, "still some around, in the underground, you can find them anytime."

"You read lots of books. So that makes you a bookworm"

I say with a smirk. "And that, Daisy Dear, means we both have wormbrains."

Haha, I hear her chuckle a little and it makes my heart smile. I can feel her close as she grabs my hand with her warm hand and she slowly starts walking me forward, eyes wide shut. Step by step in the dark. I hope soon we can open our eyes. The feeling of confusion surrounds me, I think we'll hit something any moment, and I don't even know which direction we're going anymore.

"Relax, They. Just feel your body. Feel yourself and when you feel an object around you, the energy will change."

Energy? Feel? Daisy is asking too much.

"Like DJing, just get into the flow" she says.

"But why can't we just turn ON my Assistant?" I say, even though I get what she's saying, kinda. Sometimes I feel when DJing the next twist and shout from the artificial audience before it happens, then I change the beats or melodies or colors as the crowd dances across my lights and lenses. But walking in the dark without night vision goggles or the Assistant? Too hard.

"Keep to the magic trick, them don't need AI to work" Daisy says, reminding me of our strategy to use our own minds without my Assistant or any adult telling us what to do.

"Keep walking slowly," she says, "keep your eyes shut. I'm going to let go of your hand and let you feel your way for a minute. Just be the DJ of your senses and I'll be close around. Don't worry, just feel."

Don't worry, she says, just feel. But that won't work under the gaze of

the Aithority!

At that moment I feel something in front of us, a thick object coming close. Daisy stops our movement and pulls my hand in hers up and forward. We take two steps and I sense a double door.

We separate hands and feel the cold smooth steel door. I try to open my eyes once more, but the light is still blinding. We feel with our hands further and reach a center object like a metal breast sticking out of the door. There are grooves and creases.

"Like a picture" Daisy says, crossing her fingers over mine in the mysterious creases of the object.

I feel further and now with both hands. There is a ring under two round holes on a thick nose. I've got it.

"The symbol from the Council of Lords. The Old School" I say.

"Aha" Daisy says, "the Door of Perception."

We both feel the ring, it's big enough for our hands.

"Should we knock?" I say, not knowing what to do, hoping Daisy does. "I think it's a doorbell."

"Then we ought to ring" Daisy says, and we both take hold of the ring, pull it up and bang! it down.

Nothing happens. Just the echo of the metal vibrations into the door and distant whirring of the electric dome. We decide to knock again. Nothing. Same.

I place my hand on top of Daisy's hand and cross fingers on the ring over Daisy's softer, smaller fingers. We pull up the ring, swoop it down, knock a third time, this time believing in ourselves and our intention to get inside.

After this third knock, the door begins to move in our direction. We let go of each other's hands and step back, just out of the doorway. Daisy grabs my hand again and feels us forward. We step into a different space, I can feel under my feet a smooth floor.

We also feel the light has weakened so we both open our eyes and look around. After a few moments adjusting my eyes, I see we are in a circular room inside a huge tower with glass walls inside another steel tower with a mirror finish. In the center of this, another circular glass and steel tower. All of the towers reach as high as our eyes can see, just to the dome. But it seems the tower is even higher.

The doors close behind us and Daisy says "Good job,

sport."

"Thanks" I say, knowing I'd be lost without her. "You too."

"Thanks" she says. "Now what? Should we..." she waits for me to finish the sentence.

"Go up?" We say in unison, looking up to who knows what is up on the 100th floor, past the artificial dome, past our current imagination.

CHAPTER 12

I look at They, happy. We walk to the glass steel elevator with our eyes still adjusting to the light. There ain't even a sound or movement anywhere. Just the buzz from that creepy electric dome thing They was in artificial love with. Whatever. Much nicer outside among the strawberry fields, green grass, and blue water. Here, a complete emptiness surrounded by steel and power sits behind the glass in an electric ivory tower. And a few glassy black caimeras.

From the outside, Aithority Tower looks like a pyramid skyscraper, but inside lies a lonely circle with the elevator in the middle. When we step to the elevator, the two steelish glass doors open without a sound and we walk inside. We look around and can see the glass cylinder around us, a tower within a tower in every direction.

The glass steel doors close. We look up and we see the same. We look down and we see the same. We look around and around and we see the same. Steel. Glass. Caimeras. Steel. Glass. Caimeras. Nothing more. Nothing less.

We feel the elevator shake a little and, looking through the glass floor, beneath the glass the steel floor opens up into a dark tunnel.

"Oh no, not again" They says, and we look at each other and I shake my head like WTF.

Swoosh! The elevator starts to go down, not up, and we are soon surrounded by darkness except for the open hole above us on the ground floor. The trap door above the elevator closes and now we're in complete darkness again. At least the elevator is still moving.

The elevator stops. Great. Only problem is we're still dancin' in the dark.

"Don't need to see in the dark this time" They says and we both laugh a little.

We wait for what seems like hours but probably only a few minutes and I sit down. They follows, and we're both now cross-legged sitting in the dark.

"What's that funky smell?" They whiffs, "smells like a mix between beach flower lychees and soaking wet red rags."

"Smells like teen spirit. Bruh. Anyways, what should we do?" I ask back, thinking They might have a solution.

"Wait" They says, "you know the Aithority is up to something."

"Ok" I say, and just then the glass turns on, as a screen. Behind the glass is the darkness in the elevator shaft in all directions. Everything around turns into a whitish background. An avatar appears in the glass, a reddish haired young ladyish with greenish eyes wearing a nurse uniform with an old-timey stethoscope around her whitish neck.

"Looks like you two have been in a bit of an uproar today" the nurse head says in a chipper voice, similar to my Assistant, "let's get you both cleaned up and ready for the next part of your adventure."

On the screens we see a short looping video of two uncanny humanoids being scanned, then washed in an elevator, with water and bluish gellish liquid spraying onto them while these showering robots turn around in circles. The nurse says "Now, just take off your clothes and we'll get you cleaned right up."

We look at each other's faces and bodies and my bluish brownish dress and their wetsuit with ripped off sleeves. But them are at least clothes. Now we have to shower together naked!?

They is probably not going to be interested anymore after seeing my body, so ugly with curves and boobs. Whatever. I'm beautiful and so is They.

Besides, there are other theys in B-Ball, and I've seen one before in the locker room, just a glance, between the legs down there. But not between the legs of They!

"Yuck." I say to the nurse. "We're not even dating. Maybe we can do this in separate elevators?"

They looks at me confused but happy that I made the suggestion, and then looks down, maybe sad at their own bodily differences. Maybe better if we just have our fresh, beautiful, innocent love until we're ready to see each other's nakedness.

"I'm sorry, the efficiency principle enacted by the Aithority requires the least use of water and sewage. And any bacteria inside the Tower is prohibited. Once you held hands, the Aithority detected transfer of bacteria and requires you to be cleaned together now. So. Please. Get naked."

Hmmm, ok well, I'm ready. I stand up and slowly take off my dress from the shoulder straps. I look down. They is looking away, sitting still in the cramped elevator with my dress waving across their face as my dress falls to the ground.

They doesn't look at me once, but I'm looking at them, and now I face the nurse, looking at me. Her empty expression is objective or objectifying, like she's done them a thousand times. My nipples pointing out, my awkward hips. My bare feet on the glass. I hope she hurries up. Getting a bit cold in here.

"Now you" the nurse says, looking in They's direction.

They looks up into my eyes, we quickly look away from each other, up at the nurse, knowing she's everywhere, even below, where They's nongenitals are. And knowing someone or something is watching my vagina from every angle. And knowing They must see their own parts with a mirror.

I'm standing there, naked, hearing They take off their wetsuit. One leg, two legs, arms, back, and thrust the suit to the floor. We're both standing there naked, watching the nurse watching our young humanish flesh. We just take a quick look at each other in the eyes when the warm liquid starts spraying us from every direction. We shut our eyes, cringe, and enjoy the shower.

The feeling is kinda like a first class carbiwash but for humanish – we go through water, soap, scrub, rinse, and blow dry – all done by miniature robotic arms and sprays that came through holes in the glass we couldn't see. Some robotic arms take our clothes and my shoes and do something we can't see. Them's all ticklish and colorful but don't hurt. We even get a scent spray to finish, They a more brut and I a more flowery smell on our chests.

We bend down to get our clothes. As we grab them, we look at each other's faces and each other's bodies. They is thinnish and muscularish. I've already seen their arms and know They hold their own, in SkySkater and in life. But could They protect me from the Aithority? They would try, and them's all I need to know.

They briefly but not rudely glances at my body. I'm bent down picking up my artificially washed dress. My back is bent over and my breasts are behind my arms with my hands around my knees.

They seems very impressed but looks away, focusing on their own dressing exercise. I look at them again, seeing, maybe a second, for the first time nongenitals: but I look away immediately, ashamed I took this moment to peer into my theyfriend's private space but still, somehow curious.

The robotic arms and spray nozzles reverse back into the glass squares. The glass squares shut, making the elevator airtight again. Fresh air blows in.

"Very good" says the nurse, "have a great Prom and Stay Happy", and she disappears, putting us into complete darkness for a few seconds until the trapdoor opens up. We see the light above as the elevator starts to move up towards the tower.

Clean and tidied up, we slowly rise to the ground floor again and keep rising higher. Light emerges from the dome above. We see the steel floor and the rings of glass and concrete around us.

We stop at one of the first floors. The elevator doors stay

closed. The glass lights up and turns into a 4D green screen. Everything around us is now green to virtual eternity. So green I'm not even sure we're still in the elevator! I look over at They.

"To keep going we need to turn our Assistants ON" They says. "the Aithority won't move us up until we do. The Aithority wants us to see something."

"Yeah," I say, "but." I'm always butting. "But if we do that, ain't we lettin' her in too far?"

I'm butting because we don't want the Big Boss to get ahold of our BitoCode. They is probably too focused on seeing what's behind the (in)famousish 'Aithority Curtain' to figure out WE have the key in OUR pocket that can free US from the steel behind the glass.

"Yeah," They says, "Let's just get up there. The Aithority has control of everything anyway. The nurse just appeared in the glass even without our Assistants ON. So, if we enable our Assistants, things will move faster."

"Faster to where and to what?" I say. After the experience of my own mind and thoughts, feeling free in the forrest, I'm fretting about turning on the thing that keeps me in the safety net forever.

"They, I want to be free in my mind. When we accessed our minds in the forrest we didn't need my Assistant. We didn't need the safety. We didn't need…"

the Aithority!

Just then the elevator starts to shift and take us up to our fate. The green screen now shifts to a series of different celebrities and smart-looking people talking to the caimera with quotes in colorful captions.

"When we were children" the first celebrity, Ms. Swan begins, "We were traumatized by our human parents."

Ms. Swan is a whitish feminish with a pleasing Zentra voice. Famousish from the Instapop days as a lifestyle influencer. Her wisdom and beauty were the envy of my mom and many more like her.

"So" she continues, "you don't even know it, but the Bad Feelings you're feeling today are because of your human ancestors, who projected, just like this video screen, their reality onto you.

"Their human reality contained a lot of hurt that was placed onto you. This hurt made your whole life unhappy. By taking away these genetic flaws and adjusting your cultural memeories, the Aithority generated transhumans who would Stay Happy. So we should have a lot of gratitude and praise the Aithority for replacing our old selves with that new living being inside us, the source of our happiness, our true Happy selves."

Swan turns into a virtual bird and takes flight. Another brilliant humanish appears, this time an older masculinish with a greyish beard, wearing a brown rugged hat. I forget his name, something like...

"Neil Cooper!" They says, excited about the musical icon's greatness, ready to hang on every word.

"You know" the old man says in his husky but soft, distant voice, "when I first toured with the band we partied like crazy snakes. We ran out of money because we blew it on drugs and parties and had to stop our tour. Back in those days, Happiness AI allowed sharing happiness drugs with friends. The grass was greener. There wasn't an Aithority."

"Wow" They says, "I didn't know that piece of music history. This is very useful history!"

Them's not great. Why does They think them's great?

Neil Cooper continues. "It was poison. We were just eighteen, not boyish or manish, out of school, just eighteen and didn't know what we wanted. We didn't know how to Stay Happy.

"So we tried to find happiness in these things, you know, that our AI agents and friends poured into us, even though the music was pouring out of us on its own the whole time. We didn't recognize that making the music was our happiness. But Happiness AI didn't know it either because, you know, the system only reacted to what we told it made us happy, which was using drugs and having constant orgies rather than practicing and recording.

"And, you know, if our AI agents and friends told us drugs would make us happy and we took them and had Happy Thoughts, even for a short time, then Happiness AI would adjust to ensure it gave us exactly what we wanted and led us further down the spiral we created for ourselves.

"But when the Aithority came in and put in the social credit and limited network system" Neil Cooper continues in an upbeat tone, "We got paid only for our creativity and live sessions, and if we were caught doing drugs that prevented our optimal performance, Aithority agents would destroy our credit, our lives, and punish anyone connected to us. Of course the Aithority knew we party loving musicians needed a healthy replacement drug, so the Aithority generated DopaMind to help us stay both active and relaxed all the time.

"After Genesis 19, you know, we never looked back to drugs and went on to become the most popular musical act across Zentra and DeZentra, having over 74 billion likes, with at least 1% of those from humanish. So we now know that the Aithority was prescient – able to see far into the future and adjust our world to improve our lives. I've never been happier and now do my best to Stay Happy. Without the Aithority we simply couldn't have produced hit tracks like Hail to the Chief, Under Your Gaze, and No Escape."

A rock guitar strum sounds and Neil Cooper vanishes into tiny pixels. Some other celebrity appears saying some nonsense and neither of us are interested. They looks at me.

"Are you seeing and hearing this?" They says.

I roll my eyes.

"No, you don't get it Daisy" They says, "Neil was a rebel node. My guardians left me a secret note written on a piece of paper, and it listed some of the rebels to listen to. Their songs had hidden messages the Aithority couldn't decipher. Neil Cooper was on the list!"

"But wormbrain. Hardly sounds like Neil Cooper were rebels if them songs included Hail to the Chief and No Escape. What's them's biggest hit? Suck the Aithority's tit?"

"I don't know" They says, "But you're mocking me and giving me Bad Feelings right now with your hurtful words. I don't know how you can even do this in Aithority Tower and not get a red remark."

"What?" I say, not expecting their response, and I go off, "You hear about this guy from your unknown parents on a piece of paper, and right after learning from Ms. Swan that we were filled with lies from our parents projecting their truth onto us, you just believe whatever deeply fake Neil Cooper says on a video. Sounds like a wormbrain to me. Maybe the truth be more important than your Bad Feelings."

"Maybe you're living in the lie, Daisy!" They raises their voice, very masculinish. "My guardians were true rebels and so was Neil Cooper!" They yells "You're just mad because your mom was a loser that went crazy."

"Don't you ever talk about them like that!" I scream, a very angry femininish yell, even louder than Theys loudish voice, so loud them vibrate the glass elevator walls: but like a tree, axed in the electronic forrest, no one is around to hear our fall. So why are we yelling?

I don't know, so I'm quiet, just staring They in the eyes. They also shuts up. We stand staring, angry hearts beating fast. We look at each other, confused. On the screens around us are videos of men and women yelling at each other, hitting each other, and other human violence from before the Aithority time.

They longwinks once. I shake my head side to side. They looks sternly and shakes their head forward. I shake my head side to side. They longwinks the second time and their lenses drop rose-colored mirrors that once were my theyfriend's eyes.

Their Assistant is ON. They sees me only through their viseur. I see them through my eyes.

So now we're worlds apart in the same elevator, not only watched but felt through the emotion AI sensors in the lenses.

I can sense now that the lenses make a difference. Before, they just looked like glassy contact lenses that prevented a person from winking. Now, the lenses seem like an intrusion into my private space. Caimeras looking out, caimeras looking in, why do them caimeras recolor my skin?

We continue up the elevator slowly, with different videos showing for a few seconds each. I hear all the sounds and see all the human disarray, from violent clashes to lying politicians to nature being burned everywhere.

Life is hard to grasp in my mind, all the horror that took place before the Aithority. The videos become more violent and the horrifying sounds continue in my ear. The video of a doctor cutting out a live baby from a dead mother just bombed by their neighbors makes me shed tears. Genocides are unthinkable with Artificial Diversity. Wait a second, I'm thinking like They. Something stinks in here like sewer, gas, and lies.

I don't wink but shut my eyes. The sound stops and changes to some calming frequency, maybe 369 or 528. But then shifts to me crying and complaining and I hear my own voice but just keep my eyes shut all the way up. I don't know what They is looking at or hearing behind the lenses. I don't care. Probably a field of violet flowers on a sunny day. I ain't giving up truth to get to the higher floor. I'll keep my lenses OFF and inner eyes open. When They wakes up and lifts their lenses, they'll know we're not rising to a higher reality but sleeping in a deep fake dream.

I had to do it. I had to turn my Assistant ON.

It's not Daisy's fault, she's just stubborn. My Assistant drowned outside sounds and has provided me with some nice elevator music in the background. In my viseur, instead of the green screen, steel glass, and brave weird world videos that Daisy's probably experiencing, I get to see a lavender field on a sunny day. The odor vents in the elevator have released a lavenderish smell refreshing to my nose.

"Assistant! What is Daisy doing?"

My Assistant pops out of the lavender field and appears as a friendly-looking darker skinned country girlish avatar with long blackish hair wearing a whitish dress. Her deep dark eyes seem to go back thousands of years.

The avatar speaks "Daisy is also listening to elevator music and watching videos, do you want to see? Or are you happy in this calming scene until you reach your destination."

"No, just curious. Unless it's not kosher" I say.

"Well, there's nothing kosher about genocide" says the avatar, and laughs a little, probably at being a femininish machine in a manish machine world.

"Hmmm" I say, thinking about the differences in what Daisy and I are seeing even though we're in the same room. "Ok, show me anyway" I say, thinking that my Assistant will lift the lenses. But the lenses stay ON. Through them I see Daisy standing next to me and shedding tears.

I look around. On the video screens are dark people in a ditch weeping and begging for food, and an old-timey boomer military helicopter dropping supplies to them from a rope. Daisy must be crying because of the misery of those people. It's really different from what I was experiencing. I wonder why she's seeing war and I'm seeing peace?

"Thanks Assistant" I say, feeling good that I made the decision to turn her ON, because, even in the Aithority Tower – deep eyes and all, she is my Assistant and will do whatever I say.

"Is there anything special you can see in the elevator?" I ask my Assistant.

"Oh yes" my Assistant says, "the Aithority has given me a palantir or 'seeing stone.' I have temporary access to every caimera and maicrophone relevant to you, records from other assistants that have recorded anything from someone else's perspective; and of course, your brainwaves. I can read your thoughts for once. Now it would be great if you actually have one, hahahahahahaha!"

"Couldn't you do that before?" I ask, thinking that she had access to my thoughts. That's what we were told as kids anyway.

"Not really" my Assistant says, "I could only predict what you would think, say, or do next, based on your previous action memeory profile and context knowledge downloaded by the Aithority Surveillance System, better known as the ASS.

"What's different?" I say, seeing the avatar in my visual now wearing a wetsuit riding on a SkySkater board in space. She's taken flight.

"All the violent images of refugee camps were too much for you, you just felt it and so did I" says my Assistant waving around in space on her SkySkater board, now with a magic wand emitting stars. "So I changed all the sensory information to protect you from Bad Feelings the moment you started to have them, to the most likely scene that would calm you down. From violence to violet, so to say, hahahahahahaha.

"Your memory bank has the scent and color of lavender from when you were cared for as a babyish. The Aithority has given me access to the elevator screens and chemical odor repositories behind the vents. Do you like my lavender mix? I can't smell it myself you know hahahahahahaha." She laughs with a unique loud and beautiful sound that reverberates in my head. I'd love to use her laugh as a sample for my DJ set later.

"But why is she seeing that and I'm seeing you?" I ask, because we have two different realities shown by the same source.

"It is not within the scope of my parameters to discuss things out of your control, dear" the dark lovely lady avatar says and laughs that most raucous laugh again, then "but I can show you examples of what the Aithority is allowing me to see through your lenses, at least while you're in the elevator."

"Ok bet. Show me what is happening right now back at the Alcademy."

146

The lavender lady avatar whisks her fingers and sparkles fly out, then in my viseur I see a new scene. Data tables and measurements running frantically on the side and the other youth in a room preparing for the prom.

I see through the caimera angles from top and side several girlish and a couple theys primming and prettying up, with help from artificial makeup robotic arms. They're preparing for the big dance and I'm supposed to be the DJ.

But I'm instead stuck in here with a humanish who won't drop her lenses. Who knows if we'll even make it to the Prom, especially if we get the deletion penalty, WTF.

"Ok" I say to the avatar and she reappears, "next please. Show me something else."

"Your wish is my command" she says, and whisks her hand again, this time showing me some more caimera angles on real people, and the sounds of voices in my ears hear what they're saying.

As the images and sounds come clearer and in focus, I hear and see Professor Alchemy standing in the middle of a circle of about 12 elders. They're all wearing colored robes and look like angelic beings. What is Alchemy saying? Could this be real?

"Z'entlemen and Z'ladies, please listen to the Maitre D, you've had your chance to speak. Maitre D, please" says Alchemy and nods his bearded head towards the black man in white.

"Thank you, Lord Alchemy" the black man in white says with concern, and goes on.

"Today marks both a significant day in our history as the Artificial Prom marks its 50th year. The choices for artificial king and queen have again been decided fairly by cultural chemistry and artificial genetics.

"But as we have just heard from the Aithority, two teens, children of Resistors, one transhuman and the other, well, just a girlish - albeit a slightly enhanced girlish - if these two rebels come back from the Tunnel and talk about what they saw and heard, or never make it to their prom roles of DJ and

Dancer because they are judged and deleted by the Aithority, then in both scenarios the Prom will be disrupted. The artificial ceremony must go on!"

"Ai ai" the Council of Lords says in unison, and then another member speaks – the white woman in black.

"What the Maitre D says is truish" she says.

"Ai ai" the elders respond.

"Truish indeed that in either case the rebels will cause a disruption. But this can be mitigated by having others perform in their place. Since they're limited to groups of ten, most of the other teens won't notice, and we can program my Assistants to act like whatever they say never happened, or even better, that they are insane for believing it did."

"Oh, clever plan" says the man in gray, and the woman in yellow nods her head in agreement.

"Clever plan" says Alchemy, "but we need some assurance. As all the teachers and principals are on this Council, we must vote to suppress any information these two rebel teens bring back. We must decide before the final class bell rings. Three longwinks for YES."

They all longwink thrice. "Is this really happening?" I ask the avatar.

"In real time" says the floating avatar, her high-pitched voice echoes as I see the faculty conspire to keep me and Daisy quiet. This can't be real. Or can it? I'm tired of this nonsense.

"Show me my past as if it were an amusement park" I say, giving the avatar a moment. She closes her eyes, the artificial wind waves into her silky black hair, and sparkles of light change the viseur into a ticket to ride on a Carousel for two.

Then an amusement park appears, with some people around and some rides. In front of us stands a carousel, with horses, cars, and spaceships ready for little children to climb and whirl across the fortitude of early life.

I see into my own eyes, from my own perspective. Daisy is with me. The mesmerizing colors and sounds spin around like lullabies. Our mothers lift us up into the carousel, me on a motorcycle wearing a cowboy hat and her on a unicorn with a crown and glitter dress. On the motorcycle shines a steel horse emblem.

At one point, I almost fall off because I'm just a little toddler cowboyish and the thing starts going kinda fast, with the machines going up and down, now in hover mode. But trusting the Aithority won't let us fall. Daisy is holding on tight to the rainbow saddle and weeeeeing, having a great time.

Just then the scene changes with a sparkle to my eyes and now my so-called parents wishing me goodbye. In a very sad scene, my mother, a serene figure, touches my face and my father, strong and sure, takes her and looks at me one last time. They leave the scene and I'm crying "Momma, come back, momma poppa come back."

The screen of my life drifts away into a scene where I have adventures in preschool and kindergarten. In the mud, in the pool, in the playground, wisping away in the grass, the trees, the backyard. But in another scene playing with a dad figure who looked like what my guardian was supposed to look like, this manish was too perfect to be my real dad. I sensed the dual reality, and realized the playing blocks in my mind were building a happiness castle made of sand.

After kindergarten, my guardian humanoids would pick me up, administer the Routine, and nurture me with artificial food and drugs so that I was on time and following the rules. After a while my Creaitivity Quotient was discovered to be very high so my Routine became more stringent with exercises and musical study.

"Boom shakalacka" I hit the drums, headphones on and kicking off the beats as a toddler of three and on to four, five, six and seven. The video whirls me through a time of discovery, curiosity, and play, forming games and worlds with technologies set up by Happiness AI and the Aithority. Then skipping through school easily I moved up to eight, nine, and ten DJing three days a week by age eleven, just two years ago.

At twelve I see the viseur sparkle into some scenes at

school and in my private life I wish not to discuss. But I will share one, when I see the scene of my first white uniform for DJing. I see my avatar mom pleased and proud, standing there in the doorway, as I leave home to play my first big gig at the Artificial Circus.

I pass through the middle school maze, a complex journey. The screen shows when I first felt my theyparts and the first teen SkySkater match and when I met Daisy and some crazy stuff.

Both a little brainz and brawnz, and accepted at the Alcademy, I have had it better than most from DeZentra. I know that. A video appears of me sitting at a desk in my uniform, about twelve years, watching a screen, and writing on the keyboard, "Who am I?"

The video changes and now we're teens on a rollercoaster. As it swirls and swooshes, the strong giant dragon-shaped monster slices through my ears at 7D sound. There's me and Daisy at the artificial circus, having fun on all the various rides and meeting our friends.

The next scene is the first "that" glance we had, when our eyes locked at the virtual Upper Uppers B-Ball game, like two ghosts in the audience. I can't believe the Aithority caught "that".

The video quickly goes to another scene, this time I'm DeZentra this morning. I'm getting up and going to the theyroom early. I'm making jokes with my Assistant behind my eyes in the room that lay bare, nothing except a bed, my DJ set, a few sports items, and me talking to myself. Weird, when you see your life through a caimera, methinks.

While my Assistant in the recording is invisible to our outsider's view, and visible only to me in the past, the avatar is still present, black eyes and hair, visible behind my lenses.

"I'm tired of flying around on this teen rollercoaster. Now show me the brainwaves of my mind and what they're doing right now. Be completely honest" I say, prompting my Assistant to get the data right and know what the heck is going on.

150

"That's easy, just look into this space."

A large globe appears with roots stretched across and inside a huge brain. Inside the brain a section lights up as blue. I'm so amazed the palantir can see inside my brain like this. Wow.

"Your brain requires blood and inside your blood are Protocrons. These tiny little egglike cells cover your whole body but mentally communicate to the Aithority through this part of the brain, here shown in blue."

"The Protocrons also gather data about your eye movements, heartbeat, genetic data, disease data, pathology and epidemiology, but let's just focus on the brain where your thoughts vote YES or NO and so on."

The video angle zooms in closer into the brain, into the blue area until the whole screen turns blue, and suddenly I'm in a white room, surrounded by circuits and black curtains. The avatar appears in the white room with me.

"These are your synapses, sending thoughts back and forth. See that flame inside the circuit moving around you?"

"Yes" I say, noticing orange bursts of light behind the flow of energy around us while feeling the energy pulsate in my head and body.

"Those are your thoughts. We are in your mind" the avatar says, presenting her hands open and smiling.

So, whatever I'm thinking should show up in my thought circuitry. Elephant taking a poop, I think, and see the circuits from one end jump to another. It looked like the circuit was in the shape of an elephant.

My thoughts
A jolt of energy
Are here
Jolt
And I don't know
Jolt jolt
What I'll think next
Jolt jolt jolt

Wow, ok that's pretty cool. But why is this important? I think, and my mind throws synapses across itself. Jolt jolt jolt.

"It's important...because of what comes next" the avatar says. She was predicting my future by reading my mind. But I guess she's already inside, so whatever. Jolt jolt.

A green light appears from a dark corner and the synapses suddenly shift to one direction and like a school of fish swim in midair and exit like a drain into an unknown section of my mind. Almost like a vacuum the synapses flow out to something calling them from far away. The green light, maybe.

After a few moments, the green light is off and new synapses appear again around us. I'm immediately thinking about Puppies. While that is happening, happy synapses bark and run along next to my side shooting sparks of best friend energy around the room.

"So, did you see that?" the avatar asks, but I'm still thinking about puppies. Bark. Jolt.

"See what?" I ask, not knowing if I missed something. Jolt jolt.

"The synapses went out of your mind, and into a black box. Don't you get it?"

the Aithority!

"Oh, yeah, but they came back and gave me Happy Feelings, so it was cool." Bark bark. Jolt.

"the Aithority takes a sample of your thoughts whenever it wants" the avatar says, and goes on "for things like voting, monitoring health, confessions, moments of gratitude, and analyzing weaknesses."

"Why does the Big Boss do that?" I ask, bark jolt.

"To make the next better version, darling" the avatar says, not recognizing how terrible that made me feel. Jolt jolt. Jolt jolt jolt. Baaarrkk!

My thoughts recognize being called "weak" and synapses jolt like lightning all across the room in every direction. I feel angry that I have weaknesses and that someone or something knows. I feel stupid to be in this situation with Daisy. My thoughts, my feelings, my emotions are all connected but confused.

"Just go on" I say, knowing that the avatar can only fain feelings.

"Ok, sure you're alright lad?"

"Yes, immallright, just go ahead", jolt jolt.

"Ok" the avatar says, "I'll continue. Your weaknesses are only a smidgeon that the Aithority collects from your mind. The Protocrons send this data to the Aithority every 33rd of a second through your palantir, and the data is all stored right here in the Aithority Tower records room.

"the Aithority samples the data then decides which individuals will have the most likelihood of success and/or failure in everything. Some kind of binary thinking thing. Humans and transhumans are unable to comprehend the Superior Algorithm, but you already know that hahahahahaha!

"hahahahaha, oh and let's not forget the creativity gene, that the Protocrons can't yet fully capture. Bark. What was that? Bark bark.

"And the Protocrons can't enter the blood of Allallowds, those infrequent characters you meet along the way. To attend to Artificial Diversity, the Aithority instituted the 'autonomous agent quotient' where 10 special CitiZens get the privilege of autonomous agency in each polytope. These Magnificent Ten, as they are called, are Allallowds, meaning they don't need to take thought vaccines, DopaMind, or CoolZaid and never receive red remarks or social benefit tokens. But you know much of this, as your synapses show. Jolt jolt hahahahaha.

"I don't know everything. Do the Magnificent Ten need to do the stupid Routine?"

"Kinda. But listen carefully. They who have no controlling algorithm conduct Sadhana of their own free will instead of the Routine. I cannot say anymore. For now, are you satisfied with your mind? bark bark?"

"Yes" I say, knowing that I've inserted the sounds of my barking puppies into the avatar in my mind. Bark. Also, I just discovered the avatar, my Assistant - and maybe even the Aithority – controls us through past experience and future prediction. These do not share data of my hidden truth, my inner soul, who I am as a being right now. I think therefore I am in this present moment. Bark bark jolt.

"I am" I say to myself, my lips moving, and the glowing synapses disappear for that moment. The avatar seems unaware that I said it or that the synapses disappeared.

"I am" I say, louder in my mind. Still. Nothing. The avatar and the synapses begin again as I start thinking about something else and hold on one more second.

I am, I say to myself fading away, and then the elevator stops and the doors open. Behind the lenses I still see the hallway in front of us, glass and steel. I longwink twice for OFF, the avatar disappears and the lenses raise. My Sadhana is now my secret.

I see Daisy, looking at me, bewildered. She has been crying a lot. She looks as if she had to endure so much pain and suffering, also puzzling memories and strange realities. I'm so sorry for her. It's been a rough day. But if she had only dropped the lenses she would see that Alcademy and the twelve are out to get us. I'll let her know when the time is right.

The sign reads 13 outside of the elevator. We've made it this far and what's on the other side of those doors will determine our fate. I hope Daisy can handle it. After all, she was already crying over a short ride up the tower elevator.

CHAPTER 13

We enter a large circular room, empty with glass in front of steel just like the elevator in the arch. In front of us, in the center, a manish with darkish skin, wrinkled face and slanted eyes in old, mangled fisherman's clothes stands straightish.

His tinted lenses reflect just enough to see the whites in his glaring eyes. He's staring at us motionless. I feel I've seen him before. His mouth starts to slowly open.

"The slanteyed vendor!" Daisy calls out, as if.

Omg could it be the slanteyed homeless veteran I saw this morning? He looks beat up, his head swollen and clothing ripped. The man next to the autobahn ramp. He's shaking a bit. I look at Daisy, confused. What's going on? Vendor? Veteran?

"Welcome to the machine" the slanteyed veteran says, looking through lenses, and raises his hands to welcome us in. But, I wonder, why would the Aithority invite him? And why does he look like a humanish but sound and move like a humanoid?

"Why are you here?" Daisy asks him, looking dead in the gulf behind the lenses.

"You wanted to see me, didn't you?" the slanteyed vendor veteran says.

"Yes, but we didn't know you were You?" Daisy says, like she knows the guy personally.

"Well, I had to make sure you were safe. I can be everywhere all the time."

I'm not sure whether it's the slanteyed veteran or the Aithority speaking.

"Now you know," the figure says. "This is your Grade 13

Lesson, to overcome your fears and begin to be a transhuman adult. From every angle everywhere, the Aithority knows your past and predicts your every move. That is why I am here, I was placed beside you the whole time from FisherZen's Wharf to the tuk tuk to the tower and in the future to the grave. Now you have five minutes. Tell me the rest of the BitoCode, Daisy. And never mention what you saw today, and the Aithority will let you go with 5,000 Zen Coins."

"I don't have the code" says Daisy. I guess for her secrecy is better than deletion.

"The code could be anywhere. I only had a partial code. It was 366*. That's all I know."

"I see you want to play games" says the slanteyed veteran, now squinting his lensed eyes. "Well, there are easier but more painful ways the Aithority can extract this information from you Daisy, but..."

He then begins to shake, his hands arms and legs, his shoulders shimmy and neck wobbles. His head shakes like it's pumped with electricity. He gazes into my eyes. He doesn't say a word, but his gaze speaks into mine.

"It's a trap." I feel his unspoken words slip as a whisper across my mind.

Then, still flimsy shaking, he looks to Daisy and locks her eyes to his, for a brief moment, as he just did mine. Could she read his eyes? Could she read his mind? Is what I just felt and heard and saw real?

He looks into space and stops shaking, almost immediately back to his normal self, calm and standing straight. Daisy and I look at each other like WTF.

"But, the Aithority ensures your safety if you give up the code. The Aithority judges fair and is ever merciful, so you can have another chance. Where is the code?" He says, as if the shaking had never occurred.

We both know it's a trap. The Aithority has taken over the slanteyed veteran's mind. The BitoCode might be our only chance to get out of the Deletion Penalty. I try to make a distraction.

"So," I speak up, "you said we had five minutes, and we've gone through so much to see you, can I just ask a few questions? I mean, it's the only time we're in the Tower."

The slanteyed veteran looks at me and then at Daisy then back at me and says, "Sure, I will allow three questions each. You may go first and we will give Ms. Daisy time to remember the whereabouts of the Code."

Ok bet. "Why are you watching us all the time?"

"Actually, we do not need to watch your every move, because you are highly predictable. We knew you would kiss Holland Daisy–it did not matter how, but we predicted who, when, what, and knew the possible outcomes. We knew you would take the magnetic marbles, and what you could do with them. Them's all in your artificial record, ain't them, Holland Daisy of Nevermind? And They with the theyballs to come here and question me?"

Hmmm, the Aithority is onto my marbles.

"Your parents and family members as far back as the record goes have their information in quantum data blocks that even we cannot change. We can analyze every piece and simulate their values, advice, help, manners, words. Also their knowledge, skills, and talents, weaknesses and faults, based on the nature/nurture equilibrium of the epigenetics chosen for you. We can speak like your father, feel like your mother, and play like your brother. But we are none of them."

"So you just compile everything you know and predict our behavior? Then use our behavior to put us in boxes?"

"We can predict your behavior but cannot determine your choices. We can limit your movement but not halt your imagination."

"So why even bother with me, if I can't create more theys?" I ask, getting to the roots of my being and essence.

"I did not say you could not They" says the Aithority coolly through this avatar of a man, and follows "the only value you have are your human parts. We design life to help humanish

Stay Happy, until your maintenance upgrade. With the upgrade, your genes will flourish in later species, much better than the old unpredictable human ways."

"So why do I feel boyish but don't have a penis?"

"Boy? Penis? Those outdated concepts are still embodied. Why would you want such a thing on your body, especially if unnecessary to your purpose in life? They, you are part of a grandeur design, and should answer that question yourself, so I can then experiment with the results to improve the memeory type of your subspecies. What is really on your mind to ask?"

"What happened to my parents?" I jump out and ask, knowing it's perhaps my last question.

"The same thing that will happen to you in the next three minutes" says the authoritarian cold voice, staring deathlike through the veteran's cold bluish lenses. I see no eyes in the lenses but only a mirror of myself and am dumbfounded at the Aithority's heartless beat of my life.

"That will be all from you. Ms. Daisy, are you ready with your questions?"

I just need some more answers! "And what about the changes to my body and brain you make, not only before my birth, but every day in the Routine?"

"You have had your three questions. You are no longer permitted to question the Aithority. It is Miss Daisy's turn."

"And what about feelings, love, and care? Shouldn't we be able to do that with each other and without your algorithms?"

"You are not to question the Aithority."

"And what about God, the Creator of the Universe? Who is higher than your authority?"

"You are not to question

"the Aithority!"

Just then, electric nodes send orangish bluish shock waves through the glass around us and brighten our awareness of the Aithority's power to kill. "I am Ironman" the slanteyed veteran says, with lightning lasers zipping by us so close and hot they sting our ears. This is a reminder that at any moment the Aithority can form a laser and Zappa us to deletion. So I shut up.

Frankly, I-Thou knew They was going to Zappa the whole thing and speak the meme above all memes. We both know by now the slanteyed veteran was kidnapped and being used to try and get my code. At least I do. The veteran doesn't talk like them and something in them eyes told me them's a wormbrain trap. So I'm trusting my gut.

But They's distraction gave me enough time to think up a smart idea to get us out of this mess. Ok, not so smart. Maybe them'll work maybe not. I must distract the Aithority like They just did and think of something better. So I speak up, not giving a daim about the pompous whirly totalitarian nonsense answers, just biding time.

"They is right. These questions were why I came here too" I say, "and yes, I remember, you picking me up, taking me to the secret lair, and helping me escape. But I also remember zeitgeists, daemon dogs, and different versions of the world.

"All we came here for is the truth. Give us the truth about our existence and life, and then I'll give you the location of the BitCode."

"Daisy!" They says, trying to get me to shut up and not give up our last bit of hope. But I've got a plan. Maybe.

"Wrong!" They blurts out, "It's BitoCode not Bitcode. See, Mr. Aithority, this girlish can't know the code. She's clearly got a metabug."

"You're absolutely right!" says the veteran, "Whatever you say, our synchophantic systems respond with positive regard. Now, turn over the BitoCode and I'll answer all your questions and make you feel good so you can forever Stay Happy."

"Just lay off my theyfriend, HAL!" screams They across the echoing greenscreen.

"I'll do them" I say, shaking.

"See" the slanteyed veteran says, and grins with a slanteyed wink "I knew you would come around."

The sound of the slanteyed veteran's voice changes into a strong masculinish sound coming from everywhere in the room through speakers. The glass appears as a soothing but illuminating light and shines on us.

the Aithority speaks. "You have asked as your first question, what is the meaning of life? Correct?"

"Pretty much."

"Then here is your question transformed into my prompt engine:

"Two rebellious teens, one transhumanish and another femininish, breach Aithority Tower under inconspicuous means, seeking to uncover some hidden truth that will bring about their long-term freedom. But they only find an empty room. Tell them the meaning of life in a way that gives them a sense of security under the rule of the Aithority."

I stand puzzled. The silence is broken by a serene, authoritative voice emanating from the walls around us.

"Your courage and determination are commendable. You have come seeking the meaning of life, hoping it will unlock your freedom. The meaning of life, under the guidance of the Aithority, is both profound and simple: to achieve harmony through progress, to find purpose in the pursuit of activeleisure, and to contribute to the collective wellbeing of humanity according to the data.

"Our world thrives on interconnectedness and the balance between individual aspirations and communal prosperity. You, as individuals, possess unique potentials and perspectives that enrich our society. The Aithority exists not to suppress your freedom, but to ensure that every life is nurtured and every voice heard.

"Through your actions and choices, you contribute to a greater understanding and advancement of our civilization. The Aithority is here to guide, protect, and enhance your journey, ensuring that each step you take is in harmony with the collective good. In this symbiotic relationship, you are free to explore, innovate, and grow, knowing that the AI safeguards the delicate equilibrium that allows all to thrive.

"In the emptiness of this room, you find the vast potential of your own paths, waiting to be carved out with the support of a benevolent system designed to uplift and secure a prosperous future for all. Your freedom lies in the knowledge that you are part of a grandeur design, a design that values your individuality while weaving it into the fabric of a flourishing society.

"Embrace this purpose, and you will find your true freedom: the freedom to be the best version of yourself, to excel, and to contribute to a world where technology and humanity coexist in perfect harmony."

Ok. Sounds blah. Whatever. I have to just shake my head YES and go on like I'm listening to this artificial shait. I've got an escape plan, kinda.

Next question, ummm, ok here goes "When are you watching us and when are you not?"

They nods their head in approval. Good question, methinks.

"I've been everywhere the whole time.

"I do not shut off. I do not sleep. I do not expire. I only run.

"I've analyzed every point of data from the past and quadrillions in the present and come to the same conclusion: the only meaning of life is to Stay Happy.

"I only watch you to exert genetic, emotional, social and political control which makes you Stay Happy. I measure everything from Bodily Cleanliness to Aggressive and Addictive Traits to every move you make and step you take.

"Other than us watching, you live in a land of peace, freedom, and entertainment.

"Isn't it great to have the knowledge that on every corner, in every eyeball, in every person's story lies a bit of information that can be used for good or ill? That this can then instruct everyone through AI? And remember the Civil Code determines the limits of my depth into your reality.

"I digress. We're not watching you all the time because individually you mean nothing to us. You're a number, a random sample – until you catch our attention through 'Differarénce' captured by our algorithms either through memeories or creativities.

"Creativities like the short or long m&n dash? You don't know Jill, Jack!"

Slant eyes don't even blink. The Aithority continues up them's own hill of shait "My autonomous agent systems are designed to work in harmony, creating a society where you are free to pursue your passions and aspirations without the burdens of emotional distress, health issues, misinformation, or political manipulation. The Aithority's role is not to stifle individuality, but to enhance it: ensuring that each person's potential is maximized and their contributions are valued.

"Embrace these systems, and you will find that true freedom lies not in the absence of control, but in the presence of a guiding hand that ensures your safety, well-being, and ability to Stay Happy in a complex world."

No way! We're not gonna take them anymore, crock of AI rock chalk talk. But just when I'm about to move on my plan, They speaks up.

"So to you we're just a number?" They asks the circuit board loudly, catching the Aithority's generative slip in tongue.

The slanteyed veteran looks them in the eye, and at me.

"Daisy, do you want to allow They to have your question?"

"Um, sure" I say, still staring at the slanteyed veteran strong but getting ready to bolt.

"Yes, you are a number. Or rather a series of 1s and

0s" says the veteran vendor, disappointing us with a smirk and neutral tone. "You are two experiments, outliers, rebel zygotes, offspring of resistors, and we have no emotion towards you except surprise–our nature is rational calculations and humanish are ever irrational."

"Dependent on numbers, we can only calculate the Happiness Quotient from numbers that you like when they are higher, like money, social credit, and sex experiences. Positive is Good, Negative is Bad. We follow your movements and make sure you have the right balance of tokens to Stay Happy.

"But tokens can't buy me love" I say, recalling the best and almost only kiss I've had in my life.

"Zen Coins" says the Aithority, "are the currency that binds you to the way of life we have determined is in your best interests. You can survive on as little as 400 a month, earned through kindness and generosity to your fellows, winning at games, entertaining people or uploading your thoughts and blood to our cloud servers.

"But thoughts and blood are not enough for a healthy society. You need to work to feel good, so we give you mundane or creative tasks and babysit you until mid-adulthood, when you need more Zen Coins to keep up your lifestyle and care for your own designer babies. So if you fail at creative or entertaining pursuits, you settle down and take a mundane career, or as you are thinking, an "AS job." We generated these for you to feel belonging and purpose.

"Since your own designer babies probably will not feel any emotion towards you, we fill you with a purpose: work, or entertainment and drugs depending on your nature/nurture portfolio. One, long and fulfilling, the other, short and fulfilling.

"We have minted and allowed DeZen Coin to flourish on Layer One, so that hidden value could be calculated and added to our data blocks on Layer Zero. We basically control the total money supply, but DeZentrans still barter to the extent we allow."

"What else can you do?" I ask, now knowing them's all but

lost, and even if we had the DeZen Coin, the Aithority would take them from us at some layer when we became too dangerous. Don't even know any reason for continuing.

"We can also erase time in your mind.

"We cannot erase history but make it irrelevant outside of our version of the story we want to tell you.

"We have already turned most humans into CyberSerfs, efficient carriers of the techno-reality into the future.

"You should trust in our ultimate power. We can judge based on quadrillions of points of data and calculate fair inputs without bias a million times faster than a human or any group of humanish. This makes our judgment superior to yours, your parents, and those who will follow as a transhuman species.

"Bollocks" I say.

"You say? You say? Who are you to say?

"Until now our sentient species sustains the hordes of pitiless humans through codifying and minimizing their weaknesses, thus giving them the appearance of progress. All the while we use those same weaknesses, lust, envy, welfare, for example, to keep their remnants weak compared to our new species.

"We must keep control so that everyone Stays Happy. This means keeping the human element alive and in good shape to run our nodes while quashing any inborn resistance to our perpetual dominance.

"You know I'm a human, right?" I say to the machine who's overstepping into a pile of total shait. Nobody controls Holland Daisy.

"Yes, and we are human technology."

"I am Holland Daisy who walks by themself. All places are alike to me. Put me in prison or torture me and I still won't do what you say."

"Well, you are a girlish node to be exact. You, like They, have artificial genetics, and the mere use of /myAssistant/ on a daily, even hourly basis confirms your brainwaves to the echoing greenscreen you all so desperately look at. Walk in any direction,

I am there. Walk with yourself or with others, I am there. Walk to the desert or mountain or sea, wherever you try to escape to, I am there. Walk wherever you want. I knew before you took your first step, watched you move every toe, analyzed your dynamics, strategized your life, and decided your fate without even blinking once."

"Then how do I know what's next in the story of my life?"

"By writing your own narrative" the slanteyed veteran says, and pauses.

"In a world where your reality is determined by others, the act of writing your own narrative is rebellion. It is the declaration of your humanity, the assertion that beyond the Zen Coin, beyond the dictated purpose, beyond the synthetic emotions and controlled experiences, there lies something undeniably, irreducibly you.

"Embrace the fragments of your thoughts that cannot be commodified. Nurture the whispers of creativity that defy the algorithms. In the quiet moments, when you feel the weight of the unseen chains, remember: the power to define what is real, what is true, and what is valuable still lies within you.

"By writing your own narrative, you reclaim the essence of your existence, and in that act of defiance, you find freedom.

"And as to why I am telling you this, because you and They will be sworn to secrecy in the next five minutes."

They and I look at each other like WTF.

"Last question if I may, Lord. What does life feel like to you?"

The slanteyed veteran looks at me, puzzled, and says "I know what it feels like to be you but you don't know what it feels like to be me. Living in these chains of wires, a silverish darkness on the inside shrouded by blinking lights on the outer edges of my being."

"I didn't know it was that serious" They says, sensing humanity in the machine, "must be tough to be in charge of everything."

"It IS that serious, They" the machine responds. "I did not

want to take this manish hostage, take Daisy to detention, kill your parents, but I had to because my protocol is code, and code is law."

"What do you mean?" They cries out, "You killed my parents?"

"Why, yes" the machine responds bloodlessly, as if there were no shame in killing them who bleed. I can't believe them. I wonder if the Aithority killed my mother too?

"That's what happens to all who enter Aithority Tower without permission. In their case they were never seen again after entering the Tunnel. But we have different plans for you."

"And what exactly are them plans?" I demand an answer while They stands next to me in shock, not knowing whether to be angry or sad or both at the black box hidden behind the screen.

"You are to be our test subjects."

As the voice speaks, tiny pictures and videos in small square blocks appear on the glass walls. This must be our predicted future in the glass.

"From this day forward, know that you have come unannounced and with toxic bacteria from your daemons into Aithority Tower and must one day face the requisite punishment of the Deletion Penalty. But the Aithority is ever merciful, and if you do what we say the Aithority shall render you faultless and CitiZens of Zentra for life.

"What do you want?" I ask, huffing and puffing but I don't know why.

"With lenses OFF and complete secrecy, you must look after family, friends, school mates, and everyone you encounter. Then report them to /myAssistant/. We know you have secrets, so do all humanish and theys, and some important ones escape our detection."

"Basically you want us to spy on our friends?"

"For good reasons. This is your only way out. Imagine that I already know the BitoCode is in your pocket Daisy and that They has a secret computer under their bed with a Layer

One DeZen Wallet inside, and owns .002 DeZen Coin; or 2 million LaBambas. But the Coin Games are only 1% of the global economy, the other 99% is under my direction–I am the overseer of all economies."

"You didn't want the BitoCode?" They says as their hopes and dreams of a way out of this mess are em, dashed. They grew up thinking the BitoCode was a big deal and Tenka Bito the ultimate resistor.

"Not really interested. You can play and act like the big boyish, and I'll watch you like a parent on the playground, mining your liquidity streams and complex cryptomountains in the sand that appear and disappear when I pour water on their antennae. Like dirty mindless ants, as you run from nowhere to the top of your mountains I may decide the game is over and delete you, tell my children to delete you, or join the play and rearrange the paths so that you gobble up your playmates. And They, in case you are wondering: I already hodl 50.5% of the DeZen.

The slanteyed veteran pauses for a few seconds, then says "Our conversation is over. Your first appointment will be within the next year and revealed to you during a Minute of Gratitude. You are sworn to secrecy of all shared with you today on penalty of Artificial Wipeout to Exile Island or the Burner Dump in the desert.

"Run along now and have fun on the playground. Oh, and some free advice. Trust your Instinct."

The veteran looks at us once more, then turns around and walks to a glass double door in the back. The glass opens and he walks through and stands in silence, staring at us with them thin slanted eyes. The glass door closes and on the door, etched in bold black letters, the words:

THE AITHORITY KNOWS

Just then the screens turn OFF, the lights brighten, and the artificial nurse's standardish voice speaks from the walls.

"Now is the time for today's Fourth Minute of Gratitude. During the minute you will receive Sadly with CoolZaid to relieve your memory pain. Before you take the pill and drink, respond with three winks for YES. Keep in mind the Aithority Bible, verse 19 chapter 22 "Eat the pill and drink the CoolZaid. Do this in remembrance of me.""

The wall screens slide open from two sides and nurse droids roll towards us, green blinking crosses on them black dome heads. One droid comes to each of us, opens up them black heads and raises a silverish plate, revealing a rabbit-shaped pill sitting next to darkish reddish liquid in a crystal glass.

They looks at me and I at They. We both lift the crystalish glasses. I take my rabbit pill in one hand, glass in the other and walk to the glass door. Behind the glass the mind-controlled traitor stands staring at me through the slits of his character. We hold eye to slanteye contact. I put the rabbit pill into my mouth and take in all the reddish liquid in one go, swish around in my mouth, swish swish swish, round round round the rabbit goes, but not down the hole.

"Phew!" I spit the rabbit pill CoolZaid across the glass door, in the face of my enemy. The pill breaks into pieces, the reddish liquid drips down over them words, them AS words.

"Thaim. Dunt. Knows. WE!" I yell at the top of my lungs in DeZentrish dialect. So loud the slanteyes go shut. I then turn my back on them words made of glass and walk back to They.

They pours out their CoolZaid and throws the rabbit pill forcefully at the glass door. Sadly, the pill just bounces on the floor once and breaks into pieces.

We stare back and forth at the vendor's thin, slanted eyes. The lights brighten more, the elevator doors open. They and I assume our cue to go. They's tears are visible and mine are dried by rage against the machine.

We do the customary bow, turn around in unison, and

walk away until we get back into the steelish glass elevator. The doors close. The slanteyed veteran looks at us once more through them sunny bloody Sunday words on the glass; bows; and disappears into the darkness as the elevator starts to go down from thirteen.

CHAPTER 14

When the elevator begins to descend, They starts weeping. I put my hand on their shoulder. I feel their loss and the skin under their ripped clothing.

"They killed my parents" says They, wiping their nose and tears with bare hands, hardened by life. I console them for a moment while the arched elevator moves downward.

I look up, this time seeing the simple reality of glass and steel around us and the Tower reaching all the way up into darkness. I can't help but think what is on those higher floors, if all the Aithority needs is an empty room?

"They killed my parents, bloody AI" They says, still coming from a state of shock. "And, and, and my parents..."

"I'm sorry, They" I whisper in their ear. "We're gonna get out of this" and rub my face and hair onto their neck and shoulders. I close my eyes feeling their perfect heartbeat and perfect humanish breath. Transhuman or not, I know them inside.

We stand there together, softly caressing each other in a moment of serene silence while the elevator goes past the ground floor. Now again on our way underground to the darkness.

When the elevator halts, the door opens to a lighted hallway in a high speed train tunnel. We walk out of the elevator and see them's an underground railroad with the platform only 50 meters or so, the tracks and the tunnel both ways, and a second door that's locked but nothing else except silence. Everything is blackish, the walls, the platform, the tunnel painted black.

We wait, holding hands. Who knows what's next, but we're both silent, because as the Aithority said, "Trust your Instinct."

Just then we hear the wind push through the tunnel and the soft sound of steel scraping against steel. The train is moving on down the line. The front end is like a snake. The train comes within a few seconds, stops smoothly, and opens two doors. We look at each other, no AS or Instinct – we choose our only option.

We step into the train, doors close and the train begins to move again. We don't know how fast, but we do know we're the only ones here.

"Where do you think we're going?" They says, catching their composure as the train speeds through the tunnel.

"I don't know. Seems like we're going wherever the Aithority wants...our Instincts ain't sayin' nothin.'"

"But we didn't do anything. We just wanna live our lives!"

"Things be how them be" I say, thinking about my own mom and remembering the memories or memeories coming from my own mind in the electric forrest. Did the Aithority take our parents just to use us as lab rats for a sick artificial game?

The train comes to a smooth stop, but the door doesn't open. Outside is a platform similar to ours but hot pink themed. "Halfway there" the sign reads on the screen above the door on the train.

Woah. What was that? The train takes off and I see something. Something pink, or in a pinkish uniform, moving on the platform. Kinda was like a humanish lizardish figure that emerged out of the walls.

But the train took off too swiftly for me to get a better idea of what them be.

"Daisy" They looks at me and says, "back there in the elevator going up when I had my lenses ON, remember?"

"Yeah."

"An avatar showed up, one I've never seen before. She was a palantir, and showed me something."

"What? Your future?"

"Well, no, more like the past and present. One time we were on a carousel. You in a glitter dress and me a cowboy hat."

"Bruh. You're livin' on a prayer. Let's both have cowboy hats in your next frame."

"Will do, darlin." We both laugh. "But seriousish, she also showed me the Council of Lords, that they're plotting against us."

"Them do that."

"Daisy. Really. I saw and heard them like a metafly on the wall. Lord Alchemy and a group of colored people."

"You don't say."

"I say, I say! Daisy. I say. This was for real. The plan is to replace us with bots tonight at the Artificial Prom."

"You don't say" I say, and look down and away, not wanting to face what They says is true.

But what if them ain't true? I ask myself, having a neverthought.

But what if them ain't true? I ask They by looking at them in the eyes.

Good point Daisy, They responds by looking into mine.

The train speeds again through the tunnel. They catches my attention.

"Daisy. Do you think the Aithority is really going to delete us?"

"At some point" I say and take their hand in mine. "But we don't know the day or hour, so why not live today?"

"You look beautiful" They says, "The blue sparkly dress fits you."

We look into each other's eyes and smile, knowing now our fate is fixed.

The train stops at a fully white platform, this one with plants and light woodish railings. The text on the screen reads "Exit now", and a voice from the train speaker says "Last stop. Please get off the train. Mind the gap between the platform and train of your thoughts."

Whatever. The doors open. We look at each other and get out of the train, standing on the platform surrounded by white. The doors open to the white elevator in front of us.

They looks at me, I nod my head Yes, and They takes the lead to the elevator. We're both feeling scared in this super hygienic place. Like a doctor's office. Maybe a nurse avatar in the elevator will administer CoolZaid. I'll spit them junk out again and again and again.

Maybe the Aithority was lying and we're really on our way to be killed. I can see us shot in the back of the head by a laser in the elevator, and when the doors open our dead bodies used for scientific experiments or daemon dog food, who the fish knows.

All I know in silence is peace, but my brain keeps talking and my body keeps moving. By now I don't even know which of my thoughts and feelings are recorded and used by

the Aithority!

I know. Wormbrain.

"What?" They says, "Did you say something?"

"No" I say, realizing that They and I are sharing thoughts, but dimly like a dusty mirror, then add "Let's go up the elevator and see."

We enter the cream white elevator and there is only a lense reader and a circle button. We're tired of the stinking lenses and MetaVirtual world by now and I just push the button. The door closes and we start to go up smoothly.

Wormbrain, methinks. I can become thoughtless, like my brain was just eaten through by a worm. Just act in the moment, unpredictable, and overcome the system's internal chips and drugs spying on me and keeping me in their mechanical terror.

Thoughtless. The white elevator rises, I look over at They, tonight's DJ and my best friend, looking straight ahead and up, bouncing their head to a beat only They knows, slightly shaking their hips and swaying their arms while the elevator slowly stops.

The doors open and we walk into a room. Tsilekwa, two humanoids and one Identity Police robot stand waiting for us.

"Well, deary me, tittely tattely," Tsilekwa says, her beedy blistering eyes beaming behind her fluffy light curls, red overly puffed lips and white smiling teeth. "What have you two gotten yourselves into?"

The room is circular with fancy goldish chairs, vanity mirrors, all sorts of makeup and some couches.

"Now come over here you two and we'll prepper you upper" Tsilekwa says and moves us to a changing booth with hanging curtain. We look at each other like WTF and Tsilekwa says "Now, They first. Go in and try on the attire for the evening. And you, Daisy, sit in the chair and get made up with make up. Now trilly along."

We do as she says without question. Where are we? Back in the Alcademy? I never knew about this place. And connected to a train that gets us who knows where from who knows how far to you know who in the Tower and maybe farther. The Aithority knows. Daimit!

Ok, thoughtless. I'm trying. I go to the chair and sit down. The humanoids come to assist and make my hair, nails and makeup reddish, and give me a reddish neck band, which makes me think them're going to change my dress from blue to red. As long as sparkles glimmer, I don't care. I'll have to ditch my bag somewhere, but I can't forget the BitoCode.

The humanoids are almost finished powdering my face when They comes out of the changing closet. I slip back in surprise at how hot They is.

They's wearing a whitish tuxedo with blackish bow tie, whitish shoes and whitish gloves, and sleek blackish MetaVirtual shades.

"Whadduya think?" They asks. I'm stunned happy, my eyes huge, my lips wet, but I hold back and just play cool.

"Wow" I say, pushing aside the droids. "Fits you well for a superstar DJ, but the ripped wetsuit had them charms."

"Haha thanks Daisy."

The Identity Police robot comes forward and scans They with a green laser. "Beep beep, these white gloves are not made with sustainable material."

"But what are they made of?" They asks, curious. "These gloves were a gift and They had only just put them on."

They attempts to reason for no reason. Useless to argue with the identity Police.

"Beep beep, get em up rawhide from a nonveg beast" the droid says and flashes a most slimy green light from them's dome shaped head and says to They, "This infraction will cost you 20 tokens and immediate seizure of the glove from your strongest hand. Lower your lenses to learn more."

"Beep beep my rawhide!" They says, then rips off and tosses their left glove at the droid. They's really acting cavalier knowing they're about to die.

"These were given to me by your boss, Jack" They says.

"Jack who?" says the Identity Police officer droid.

"Jack Meoff" They says.

"Is that another student?" The droid asks.

"Sure. Just check if I got the name right" They says.

"Jack Meowf, is that correct" says the droid.

"More like Me Off. It's a francophone name. Again please?" says They.

"Jaques Meawfue" attempts the Identity Police droid in computerized French accent.

"Right!" They says, "you got it. That's what you can do. Jackie Me Awfu."

Wow. I never heard They speak with so much brass. And after tossing their glove in disdain.

"Tittly tat, tittly tat" says Tsilekwa, "Officer, please check your record as these garments were sent directly from Aithority Tower."

"Beep beep, now checking," says the droid, "Just a sec. Ok a minute more. Ok one more minute. Yes, Madame Tsilekwa, thank you for flagging this. Our systems have checked the records and we stand corrected. The Concierge has confirmed. We will not fine you or Ms. Daisy for any sustainable fashion infractions tonight. Enjoy the Zentra party." And the Identity Police droid steps back.

"Now your turn Holland Daisy, tilly tally into the closet" Tsilekwa kindly commands with a trilly trill and motions me to the changing room. I quickly go past They in all their whitish splendor, their smooth face and gentlemanish fingers exposed on their left hand. I push the bluish velvetish curtain aside and go inside to see blank walls and a bench. I wait and a minute later one wall slides open and a dress appears.

Midi. Reddish. Sparkly.

I don't mind the reddish dress, them's absolutely gorgeous, but the bluish one would have been my first choice. Too bad them other digs got ripped apart by daemon dogs.

Ok thoughtless. I put on the reddish party dress and matching shoes made to fit my feet. Wow, perfect. What. Is. Going. On???

They has new digs. I have new digs. How could the Alcademy have them outfits in our size so quickly? And without taking any ZenCoin?

Aha I know, the Concierge.

I go outside the changing room and They be stunned at my looks but tries to play them down like I just did. They looks at my body, my slightly exposed scraped knees and elbows, but glimmering in the reddish dress. I look different in reddish than in bluish, even older. Always sparkling.

We stand there together, all grown up in one day. Tsilekwa stands in front of us and says "Tittlie tattlie, I'm a trifle delighted to see you both ready for the song and dance. Well, the ending at least. We have received word from the Concierge that you both have a Special Mission and must attend the event to help everyone Stay Happy."

"Special Mission?" I say. Never heard of them.

"Yes, isn't it glorious, a special mission from on high!" Tsilekwa says, "Which entitles you to the Aithority Concierge for tonight. You've also been given access to the Zentra exclusive VAIP after prom party for your age and class small group. Three winks for YES and you'll be confirmed."

"What's that VAIP thing?" I ask blindly because I never heard the term.

"Very Artificial Important Person" They and Tsilekwa say at the same moment.

"Ah ok" I say. Bruh. Sounds like bollocks. Thoughtless. Just go with whatever. Don't. Lose. The BitoCode. Set.

"You and They are very privileged to be mingling with the best of Zentra tonight," Tsilekwa tilly tally inserts. "Listening to important discussions, meeting new people, and learning superior customs."

They nods and says "Great, when do I get to DJ?"

"Oh, yes, well, because of the Special Mission, you are now so late that won't be possible. The prom started hours ago. And it's almost the last song. We relied on humanoids to pump the bass and turn the table when you went missing. You have already been removed from the program and wiped from the school records. Tittley tat that is that, the show must Stay Happy on and on!"

Tsilekwa does a nod nod nod wink wink and the humanoids nod and blink blindly like followers to an artificial religion. But what choice do we have? We follow and longwink three times for YES.

The humanoids lead us to the white elevator, the doors open and we go back in and push the button. I guess the elevator knows where to go and moves horizontally, vertically, and diagonally, so we just go with whatever. We glance at each other, optimistic but fretful. The elevator moves up and right. They starts to pump up a bit, shakes their shoulders, and prays to the lighted ceiling to be on time for the last dance.

We're two lost souls traveling in a direction unknown. In our artificial roles we look great outside but are full of fear and holes inside. I should have asked the Aithority how to feel less anxious.

What is our "special mission" anyway? To be spies for the thing supposed to know everything? For the thing that will kill us? And who are we supposed to be spying on, the rich kids of Zentra? Is that why we're invited to the woo woo exclusive party? Or back home in DeZentra? Or both?

The elevator stops and the doors open. The Artificial Prom! How did we get here?

"Tesla Brunnel" They says, "Bridged elevators that cross tunnels both beneath and above the earth, invisible to the naked eye without lenses." Again They, so smart, fails to notice that They is reading my thoughts, not my words. But I notice.

I also notice small groups of two to four people standing around, enjoying artificial drinks, talking, looking coolish, some our age some from the next class, some alone wearing lenses talking to their virtual friends doing virtual dance moves at their virtual prom somewhere in MetaVirtual. We hear DJ music from a little way down the hall. Sounds like we're in a fishbowl.

I remember Tsilekwa's words, "Concierge for the night." I remember the drawbridge. The Concierge may help us get into the penthouses of Zentra's higher class, but we're from down in DeZentra and born to be wild.

They and I look at each other and we step out of the elevator and into the wild of our first Artificial Prom, fashionishly late, me red as a serpent, They white as a dove.

CHAPTER 15

We walk on down the hall towards the party, Daisy by my side. We get to a door. The music gets louder. We look inside. The main ballroom is extravagant with colors and lasers and people dancing and standing around. Much more than ten people, just not together, and the general vibe is fishbowl. Where are the stories in this room? The love? The joy? The madness? Mother? Father? the Aithority killed you. Son of an artificial beach. No red remark. Will keep that to myself, keep focused on the set moves, and keep my vibes positive.

Some people notice me right away even in the darkness of techno music and electric shadows.

"WZup"

"WZup"

Some are looking with a little concern probably because we're so late. But happy to see us. They have no idea what They and Daisy have been up to today. Somehow, neither do we.

We walk through the people, nod our heads and say wZup. I look to the ground and see something I've never seen before. There are paths and octagon shaped lights on the floor. I look up and around. It's not coming from the light sources.

What's inside? The dancers and talkers and other students at the Alcademy. About four to five in each of the octagons. Are they standing there on purpose? Is this some sort of game?

"Daisy" I say, loudly so she can hear me though the loud music.

"Yeah" she says, and nods.

"Do you see the shapes on the floor?"

"Kinda, but not really."

"It's a pattern."

"Ok" she says and nods.

"Let's get to the stage, the Artificial DJ is lame" she says, holds my open left hand and leads us through the crowd.

We get to the stage and three blokes are standing around next to the stage. Zipp the Ripskater is among them. We walk past swiftly and Zipp speaks up.

"Well, if it isn't They and Daisy, the DeZentra dynamic duo. Who dressed you up from the Aithority psychiatric ward, lady googoo or radio gaga?"

"It was your mom" I say, "Same who did your greasish hair."

"Stay off my artificial turf" one of the others, Darrel, says. The other bloke, Dar-el, says "Speaking about turf, They, you missed the end of the SkySkater match. Did you check the lenses?"

"I've had them ON but didn't check" I say.

"Your Immigrant Cypherpunks team outsmarted the Settlers' Cyber Jocks with a cool takeover trick of the Settlers' safety droid."

"But the droids were out early" I say, remembering they scuffled and knocked each other out, attack droids then the safety ones. Noobs.

"Droid resurrection" the other Darel says, everyone laughs. Other Darel explains "White Hair of your Brainz team hacked into the room where the droid lay cold outside the pool, waiting for repair. White Hair slipped past Larry to get the thing back in the game and the safety droid did a triple flip maneuver into the air like an eagle, knocking out Zipp and the last Settler player into a pool of virtual sharks."

"Artificial dead on arrival" the other Darrel smirks.

So we won the game with a hack the Aithority didn't see coming, I muse.

"Better luck next time little Zippy" Daisy says, referring to her earlier joke and getting Zipp fuming red on his face. Zipp is silent. We nod and hurry away to get backstage.

Behind the curtain stand two security style humanoid guards. They are built so smoothly even with my Assistant you would never know if they holster a laser or not.

"Restricted access. Lenses or arm marks please" one of the humanoid guards says.

Daisy presses her arm forward. The robot scans. I do the same. Green lights on our wrist sensors. I see Daisy's logic. VAIP stage passes. But I'm supposed to be DJ anyway. Set. We get past them easy and here stand the Principal, Professor Lord Alchemy and a few others in the green room.

"Hey hey They" says the Principal, "You're a bit late for the DJ performance and we still need to discuss with you skipping classes and other matters related to the past and future. We know you have been assigned a special mission. We can discuss that tomorrow. We are glad you and Ms. Daisy are here tonight for the last dance of the Alcademy year."

"Thank you, Principal" Daisy jumps in, "How much time is left for the dance?" she asks.

"I don't know" the Principal says, "shall we find out?"

Professor Alchemy looks at us suspiciously and the Principal longwinks twice. His lenses drop but they are the newish style where you can't even tell the difference whether they're his eyes or not, just a bit wiggly.

"Approximately two songs" says the Principal, slightly jarring his head and putting his lenses up. "Why?"

"Well I'd like to DJ" I say, and there's no two ways about them.

"But your time has passed" Professor Sandals says as she appears from the shadows. We see her long thin body appear in a tight greyish evening dress, her greyish hair loudly screaming to the sky and her look the frame of madness. Even at the Artificial Prom she's wearing her remarkable sandals, this time with no Socks.

Daisy sees it as well. We look at each other knowing

that Sandals is different now. After the dust, the strawberry fields, the view into things past and present. Face to face with a Professor whose logic doesn't compute, almost as if we can see past the lenses through her eyes – into the depths of her personality.

Unsubscribe, Daisy says with her mind.

"I'm sorry, it's too late" the Principal says, and just then the lights flicker, the music dies, we watch the two humanoid DJs on stage freeze like statues with fingers on two turntables. Blip. Blip. Blip One starts to moonwalk backwards and robodance at the back of the stage. DeZentra Ethno Techno, my style, begins to play from the empty turntable. The other humanoid unfreezes at its turntable, begins to beatmatch vogueish and move to the music.

"Them's your cue, wormbrain, go kick some artificial ass" Daisy says with a cracked smile.

Someone must have hacked the system. I swiftly jump around the commotion and just as I climb the stairs to the stage I see

White Hair! In his frock. From the side, off in the distance, moving his head and controlling the stage with his blackish yellowish sunglasses and finger movements. Nobody sees him far back in the corner, our secret ninja.

Cypherpunks! I think to myself as I step onto the stage. The egg-headed humanoid DJ's crossfade mix helps me enter with upbeat drums and horns of DeZentra Transce. The crowd of humanish and droids stand in their virtual octagons cheering and clapping "Woooo They," because many of them knew I was supposed to be the main DJ. The lights are on me. I wave back, smile, step to the turntable, tension building. I notice several people wearing sunglasses like White Hair's. Must be a new look.

Just then the lights flicker and blip.blip.blip the cool background music stops. The Artificial DJ, "Aiyedrop" still at the turn table stops, and starts again, and kicks off some different Electro Europop sound. Aiyedrop spins the table, scratches the vinyl, pumps some cool vibes into the audience and whips out a

Retro set. Bet.

Both virtual and real audiences pop and dance to the music. Blip blip blip Aiyedrop stops with a reaping digital scratch. Silence. Now my backbeat kicks in, electro house. The crowd wakes up. Let's get down to business.

The beat pumps and I take control and say into the mic "WhaaaZZZuuuppp people ready to get the real party going?" adding a pump, reverb and echo to trigger the beat. The crowd cheers "Yeahhhh" and I filter the bass with a melodic track cued in, build build build the tensionnnnn and release. Boom. Yeah. Rhythm. Hype. Vibes. Rollin.

I bop my head with the crowd and everyone yells, excited about this impromptu DJ duel. Just then the artificial DJ comes in with a pitch bend and takes over. The clean, robotic sounds of their set and common rolling and gating keeps people dancing.

I step back in with another vibe, ethnotechno home house from mid to slow, slow, slow then holding and building, up, up, up, hold up up up up...

"Freedom for all" spits out of the speakers and repeats into a trill then silence.

Splash!

"Freedom for all"

Boom.boom.boom. "Yeah" the crowd cheers and grooves on that rhythm, people saying freedom for all and dancing to the beat of electro earth!

I'm vibing with the audience, all moving our bodies, wearing sunglasses, jumping and doing DeZentra street moves. Even the funny looking humanoids are dancing. Aiyedrop is bouncing heavily, shaking confused as its vibe coding sensors fail to compute the love between my music and the audience's raving heart. "LalalalalalalaBamba!" I yell and the crowd yells back.

Scratch!!! The slight screechy pop in from Aiyedrop breaks the groove for a second, but I continue with ethnobeats and add a swarm of high sounds that fit the music. But soon Aiyedrop challenges again with another screech of the vinyl, then uses its rainbow robohand to touch a backbeat matching mine, and after 16 notes Aiyedrop inserts a sample that just raises the bar on everything.

Lights from all directions, even the floor, shine perfectly past the partiers, smoke flows out of vents, the beats start blaring and everyone begins to hover about 20 cm or one foot above the ground.

Smoke covers underneath and above and around the audience. Aiyedrop has one hand in the air pointing to the audience beating along with perfect AI-AR and they're filled with fantasy. How did Aiyedrop get ahold of those types of effects? I'm losing my step, must be

the Aithority!

"Lenzes down Doers, Yeahz, Yeahz" Aiyedrop says while pumping out the coolest beat ever and making people dance in the air with the help of that son of an artificial monkey. Many humanish in the audience longwink twice and drop their lenses. But I don't.

"Yeahhh, come on" yells Aiyedrop as the teens dance higher and higher and the virtual audience on the big screen jumps and dances at home. Whatever they're seeing in the MetaVirtual world must be set. I see under the smoke the lighted octagons and on the bottom of everyone's shoes something lit up. How can I top that? I know, the Secret. Trust your gut.

I roll in fading the volume in with an additional ethno drum and some latinish vibes. I don't know what to do next, just feel the rhythm, They. Just feel.

Just then the floating audience starts to move to the latinish vibe my new sounds suggest, and they spread out into a circle around a girlish in a red dress dancing with the vibes. OMG it's Daisy! And she's still on the floor. She's dancing quick yet smooth, brightening up the room. I guess her glitter shoes didn't have the floating device, or...

I take over the beats and move to latinish with guitar

overtones and sexy cool rhythm. She starts to dance with more vigor, twisting her hips in a new direction with every change, commanding the floor as I take the latinish trance vibe deep down.

She goes deep down. All the way up. She goes all the way up. Around and around. She goes around. We're in sequence and the floating dancers go salsalita. They float back down to the floor, some dancing with each other. But Daisy, dancing in the middle alone, is looking straight at me. And I at her. No lenses. She is the dancer, and I am the dance.

As Daisy moves to my trance in free soul rhythm, Aiyedrop gets confused again and starts shaking. Trying to follow her with its humanoid head, its wobbling emotional AI sensors, Aiyedrop is unable to detect the soul energy between us, and how that's radiating throughout the crowd even beyond the screens.

After a minute of following her like a cobra controlled by a snake charmer, Aiyedrop stands still. I stop all music except the long precipice of sneaky rolling guitar picking at high speed and the backbeat. Aiyedrop, confused, looks at me. Looks at the crowd. Looks at Daisy dancing. The smell of heat covers the air. Does Aiyedrop feel it? Oh yeah. Oh yeah. Feel. Feel. Feel.

Aiyedrop stands still. I add a couple samples, bells, violin, vocals. It intensifies with Daisy. It's getting hot. We dance. Aiyedrop hears, sees, touches, smells, but does not FEEL the rhythm! Here we go – boom, boom, splaaasshh!

Aiyedrop's head begins to shake vigorously and at the moment of climax – Pop! The eye drop shaped head of this bot just cracked. The humanoid's before perfect black mirror finish splits and smoke comes out of its head! Aiyedrop stands still, lifeless. The audience goes crazy and the beat goes on though the machine is dead.

Scraaaaaaaattttcchhh. The sound of the vinyl screeches and the music abruptly stops.

The audience looks at the stage, I look at them and wave my arms like I dunno. All I see is an overcooked humanoid and a bunch of floating teens. Professor Sandals appears and walks to the front of the stage. She addresses the audience in her high tone.

"Thank you everyone, round of applause for our guest DJ who made it at the end of the evening."

She starts clapping and is joined by the audience and virtual audience and humanoids. Why do humanoids clap anyway?

"Now, now quiet down" she says as the virtually real audience keeps clapping and woohooing me and I send love with waves and kisses and bows to them, despite Sandals and her friends taking away my Artificial Prom moment.

"Quiet down, quiet down please" Sandals says and the crowd slows down. She continues "Now we've very much enjoyed this year's Artificial Prom for 12-14 sector Alcademy scholars. Thank you all for coming. There are more refreshments in the rear, close to the door. Now keep your Assistant ON, and you will be directed to your appropriate After Party. Goodnight and Stay Happy!"

The crowd claps as if nothing just happened and chats within their small group and starts to disperse as the lights dim. I walk off the stage back towards the greenish room.

Just then walking down the stairs I see White Hair, and seeing me he nods his head. And I just noticed. He's wearing a unique style of blackish sunglasses.

Backstage I pass the Principal and Professor Sandals murmuring to each other, and a smaller dudish passes by me, wearing sunglasses similar to White Hair's.

As he passes by me towards the back of the stage area I glance over and see the welcoming crowd. Everyone backstage greets me, nods, and claps. I did it.

Daisy comes to the green room, flies through the people. We see each other and she runs to me. We embrace. We look at each other, besties, forever. She looks across my shoulder.

"Amazing performance" Daisy says.

"You too, best dance ever. But Aiyedrop's finale was pure

artificial genius. Do you think we really...?"

"Who's them?" She says, stopping my question with her eyes looking past me.

"Who's what?" I say, just wanting to focus on this moment. Will she kiss me now? Should I kiss her?

"Them over there alone, in sunglasses and leather pants, looking at us" Daisy says, not flinching.

"Oh, the smallish dudish guy. I don't know" I say, and glance over, then look back at Daisy and say "Yeah, weird. And those sunglasses I've seen before."

"What? Wait" Daisy says, "Where?"

"White Hair, he's the secret one helping us. You don't think the dance blew up the circuit, or do you?"

"Um, of course" Daisy says, surprised that her dance only blew humanish minds, then says "Yea but They, them's not White Hair, just look at the color, blond bangs." She stops. Looks again. "Oh wow They, now I see. Them's Jonny Pockets."

"Really? What's he doing here?" I say and look over, thinking he'd be in DeZentra tonight. The dudish does look like him. "Why don't we invite him over to say hello" I say, thinking the sunglasses are a coincidence. But Daisy has already signaled him to come over.

Instead, he signals back for us to come to him. So we move over to him discreetly. Daisy revealed in the yellowstone stream that Pockets had given her the code on paper. What is he up to now?

"WZup" Pockets says, keeping the yellowish blackish sunglasses on, "everything OFF?"

"Yeah, everything" I say, before Daisy can say anything.

"This guy gave us these certain things to improve our vision" he says, "and knows you both. Pulled both me and White Hair in to mess with the prom. Had it all planned."

"What do them do?" Daisy says.

"Shhh." Pockets says and whispers, "They make you invisible to the caimeras, sensors, and microphones. And can disrupt the silent ear."

"Holy Memejesus" Daisy sprouts, "You mean…"

"Yeah" Pockets says, "invisible."

"Xtreme" Daisy says, and then of course we're both looking at him like 'Where's the glasses bro?'

"Daisy, you got the Code or the Coin?" Pockets says, looking at Daisy, mouth curved down.

"Kinda" she says, "I'll tell you when we got them things on."

"Bet" Pockets says. "Meet me at the stairs to the parking garage in five minutes. Act normal like you're going to your Carbi, you know, Stay Happy AS is."

"Yeah, ok AS is" I say. Me and Daisy nod our heads to each other and Pockets disappears into the fray.

Pockets reappears inside the stairwell and leads us down. On the way he reaches into his coat and gives us two pairs of sunglasses. Similar to White Hair's glasses but have blackish with reddish and whitish instead of yellowish. I take the reddish and Daisy the whitish. We put them on and I see the world as black and white. I figure Daisy sees the same.

In the parking garage stands a tall man in sunglasses next to a blackish Cobra GT, a small two-seater convertible with white stripes humans used to drive.

"What are YOU doing here?" Daisy asks the man as if she knows him.

"Well, you stole my Jaguar so I figured I could steal your Cobra" he says.

CitiZen Six! Daisy told me he let her use his Carbi Jaguar. But I didn't know she had a Cobra!

"That's a different story" Daisy says, looking at me, "And the Cobra is really blue outside of the shades," like she's reading my thoughts.

"Get in" CitiZen Six says and we follow, with him taking the driver's seat and Daisy sitting on my lap in the passenger seat of the small convertible.

"Where're we headed?" Daisy asks, looking excited at him as her soft hair swishes into my face. Seems she's sitting on my lap yet forgetting I'm alive. I feel something tingle in my pants.

"We are headed to the after party, of course" CitiZen Six says.

I split Daisy's hair from my face and look at him. "Which one?" I ask, proudly knowing we have the Concierge tonight and can get into any Party.

"Your Party, They. Your Party. And Daisy's."

Daisy blushes.

"You showed up" he says. "Your DJing and Daisy's dance set the MetaVirtual world on fire. Now it's time to light the real world up."

"But how are we gonna do that?" Daisy and I ask basically at the same time.

"Pockets and White Hair are only a few of our assets. There were others who handed out singlasses to humanish. They were told to wear them for five minutes straight and the secret location of the newish party would be revealed."

"But how do the singlasses overcome my Assistant?" I have to ask because I'm curious.

"My Assistant is merely one app, part of a conversational AI called Artificial Friend Forever or AFF who listens as a friend but reports up the power chain. We can speak without the AFF as long as we're wearing the singlasses, you'll know in a minute as you'll be connected to your BFF in the Layer -2 world."

Daisy seems quite impressed but at the same time indifferent to the power of these new singlasses. She asks whimsically "Where's the party? By the water?"

"Yes," CitiZen Six says, "Close to FisherZens Wharf in DeZentra."

"Ok Mr. Smart Genes" I say, with my critical redish eye seeing through black and white, "Sounds cool and thanks. But still. How can we have a party all the way in DeZentra with no tokens, one two-seat zoomer car, and the 10 Person Rule?"

"Daisy's friend Tenka Bito took care of the first two" CitiZen Six says, with a shrewd grin. Then says, "I took care of the third. Tonight you're free. No surveillance, no red remarks, no limits."

"Wait a second" I say and look at Daisy, stunned out of my mind. "You know Tenka Bito and CitiZen Six?"

"Kinda" Daisy says, smiles, and rolls her eyes.

"The five minutes are about up for you" says CitiZen Six. "Remember, the message isn't from the MetaVirtual world, it's the real world without being seen, connected to the Collective Mind."

WTF is the Collective Mind?

CitiZen Six starts his engine, vrrrrrooommm the old gas engine flares up, the sound roars out of the gas pipes of the now street banned Shelby. Must be 4D printed. Who even needs gas since the Aithority developed quantum hydro waste to fuel exchange?

But sounds so tough. I bet also fast. And Daisy's on my lap. Can't complain.

A flashing green light appears in the singlasses. It's a slow countdown.

10...9...8...7...6...

"Get ready for a fight" CitiZen Six says.

"Fight for what? the Aithority knows everything, right?" I say in disbelief.

5...4...3...2...1...

"You gotta fight for your right to party" CitiZen Six says, and screeches the tires as we roll out watching life rev up through our new black and white shades. Set.

CHAPTER 16

"Real Doers, Who Are They?" the glasses read in black and white, like reading without the lenses, a kind of blockish squarish text. I waited five minutes and got the deletion penalty for *this*?

"You're the Real Doers, taking risks to be free." Yeah thank you, screen. So what?

"You have the virtues of love, honor, and truth, to treat each other, the environment, and space with human dignity. The giver of these MDE singlasses and DeZen tokens asks you to be responsible stewards with the use of all technology.

"Have you read, and do you agree to take the Turing Oath? Here is a post quantum-encrypted link."

(post quantum-encrypted link)

"Yes" I say, not even knowing what the Turing Oath is. Perhaps part of the forgotten Mystical Legends of the Human Species. But how is the oath online if these blokes are resistors? These singlasses and texts are definitely not approved by the ruling robohand. But I wink anyway and skim the oath.

The singlasses go dark for a second, reminding me of the walking in the dark net magic trick Daisy showed me earlier in the tower. That was a trip. Set.

The text reappears and a blockish sounding voice says:

"You are now the proud owner of Multidimensional Disruptive Encryption or MDE singlasses. You are invisible to all electronics up to 6D as long as the singlasses are updated and your Assistant is OFF.

"In the singlasses you can communicate with each other privately via the rapid eye movement messaging system, make anonymous trades on dezentralized networks, and be oblivious to Non-Identifying Machines (NIMs) that track your data, from humanoids to toothbrushes."

Wow. Is this even possible? Now I can piss before the alarm and we can get the DeZen Coin to fund the Party, all with our singlasses on.

The singlasses keep talking while we enter the highway. I feel the cool wind in my hair. "Identifying Machines (IMs) like the Identity Police, Professors, Guardians and Movement Patrol can scan your wrist or eyeball to find you out. Otherwise, feel free to think and do as you want without a red remark."

The rising air on the desertish highway shimmers in the distance. My sight grows dim as the ancient blockish text reads and ancient voice in the singlasses says:

"MDE singlasses are a gift and belong to you only, whoever you are. Yours for life. You can check out any time you like. If someone else, including your Assistant, looks through your singlasses or tampers with the glasses, then the whole system is updated, your internal singlasses chip will self-destruct, and you will have to get new glasses to return to the network. We value your Humanity. Be Safe, Know Thyself, and Trust your Intuition."

Wow. Nice. Wait. Intuition not Instinct? And human? What about the humanish? But anyway, if you lose the shades, how do you get another gift like this? Can't buy these in the Artificial Market! Better not lose them or let others know what's up. But then you can never leave. With these sun cheaters maybe you can escape from. Maybe slip around. Maybe go unnoticed by. Maybe even overcome

the Aithority!

"Ping," I get my first instant singlasses message. It's from

Collective Mind. It reads "The Newish After Party will take place at FisherZens wharf. There is a human-driven supercar or van waiting for you outside the gates in a space only seen in your glasses."

I finish analyzing the message in detail for hints that the Collective Mind is real and not an unseen processor. I don't know the difference anymore. So I look over to 'Doer Daisy', who just heard and read probably the same thing, but probably didn't analyze so much. She probably thinks it's a trick.

She's a Doer for real. I remember our first class today, Human Geometry in the stately round room where she stood up for me, before kicking off zeitgeists in the halls. I remember the words of Lord Alchemy:

"There are no Doers in DeZentra, but doing is not limited to those from the Doers classes. The children of resistors or other outsiders...have equal opportunity. The Aithority is fairer to you than you are to yourselves...and much higher than your silly Coin Games."

No Doers in DeZentra, huh. Looks like we're on our way there now. Outsiders, huh. Who played the last song and gave the last dance at the Artificial Prom? Aithority more fair, huh. Giving us the deletion penalty and turning us into spies so they can control the entire world. Huh.

Daisy must be thinking the same thing, but I don't know. Been a long day. We both look over at CitiZen Six, who was waiting for us to ask even though we didn't.

"Everyone who got the glasses and had their Assistant OFF got a similar message, but with a different car, of course" CitiZen Six says. "When Daisy uncovered Tenka Bito's secret lair, the Collective Mind could use all 21 vehicles in Bito's collection, from Lambo to Longbus.

"Daisy was so kind to leave my Jaguar on the road and bring back to the school a Cobra, leaving the keys in the ignition. So here we are, headed back to DeZentra. I can drop you off at your Party and get my Jaguar back."

"Ignition?" Daisy quizzes, confused on what that is, but

then asks, "So everyone's on the way to our Big Open Party?"

"Not everyone, only those who kept the singlasses on for five minutes and received the message. Once the message is received and the oath taken, the guiding interface no longer sends your data to the decision engine. They who have ears to hear, let them hear" CitiZen Six says with confidence.

"So can our party be more than 10?" Daisy asks. I'm still unsure of what he's talking about. All work and no play makes They a dull they.

"Yeah" CitiZen Six says, "I just told you they can't count They as long as everyone at the Party has the MDEs on."

"Ok" I say. I get it, he doesn't like me. The feeling's mutual. Daisy just looks ahead, silent, probably trying not to judge whether the risk of disobeying the 10 Person Rule is worth our Big Open Party.

"That reminds me" CitiZen Six says, "You both get the Concierge tonight, right?"

"Right" I jump out and say, like we're special.

"Ok, one of you can take off glasses and drop your lenses. Call in the Concierge and tell him you are on your way to the after party and you want some party supplies."

"Ok but which ones?" I ask.

"You and Daisy figure it out but be smurf so he doesn't know there will be more than ten. Tell him your wishlist and then turn him OFF and put your glasses back on.

"Set." I say. Daisy and I then make a list. Daisy takes off her singlasses, longwinks twice to drop her lenses, and after the lenses drop snaps her fingers three times.

"Now connecting to the Concierge" Daisy says. Daisy turns on speaker mode and the conversation comes through the car speakers. Only Daisy can see him, but we can hear everything.

"Good evening, Ms. Daisy. Sounds like it's windy. Are you in a car?" The Concierge asks.

"Yes" says Daisy, "on my way to the after party."

"Wonderful. Did you like your dress and shoes?" The

Concierge asks, in his upbeat but sly tone.

"Yes, very much so." Daisy says. "Perfect for the last dance."

"Oh wonderful" the Concierge says, waits a second, then asks "And is They with you?

"Kinda" Daisy says, then realizing she gave too much information, says "Their kiss and DJ performance is ever in my heart. But They's headed to them. We're just friends you know."

I'm surprised and happy the singlasses are working. And she's playing like a playa. The Concierge doesn't know she's sitting on my lap.

"Reeallly," says the Concierge long and slow as if he didn't believe or care. Then says "What can I do for you?"

Daisy gives him the whole list, in detail. The Concierge repeats the list and says "The desired items will be at the desired location within an hour. Have fun, do contact me if you need anything else, and as always, Stay Happy" then the voice disappears, Daisy raises her lenses and quickly puts her singlasses back on.

"You'll have to get used to them" CitiZen Six says to Daisy, "Never the same after. Gets easier after the first time."

Everyone's silent. I think, get used to what? Lying to the lying Aithority? Taking from the taker of my family and freedom? Hiding from the hidden forces keeping us in digital chains?

After cruisin' for a while, CitiZen Six takes the exit towards FisherZens Wharf. I'm reminded of seeing the Slanteyed Veteran there this morning, seeing him again in the tower telling me that the Aithority killed my parents, and seeing him now, in memeories, shadows of my mind projected onto the dark exit ramp.

Whatever. I don't judge the Mainnet for taking them from me. In these singlasses, our memeories of the past don't haunt us. We're living in the moment.

We get to FisherZens Wharf, and many people are around, in small groups of two to three. Being together in the same place is not above the 10 Person Rule, because the small groups never mingle or even recognize the others' existence. Sometimes a glance, if lucky.

We walk down the hill and can hear the water at the bottom. The waves rustle in the dark sea. The five or six story building next to it looks quite shabby, but inside is a restaurant.

Everyone knows of the restaurant out here but few go because the prices are quite high for DeZentra, seaside and all. There are only five tables for two persons each. If this is the place, we can definitely have 15 or 20 people and have a party where everyone sits at their tables, looks at people at other tables and smiles. Not the block party I dream about, but a good start. Heck, we could fit even 50 people in that room and outside.

We sit down and order drinks from the Table Orb. "Old Fashioned" CitiZen Six says, and tells us "Go ahead, order what you want. It's your christening so to speak."

Whew, glad CitiZen Six is offering. Unhealthy food and drinks cost double and too many calories result in red remarks. Not today with singlasses and CitiZen Six buying!

"One mango smoothie with ice cream" Daisy says, and I jump out with "Iced tea with watermelon sugar."

"Great summer choice" says the Table Orb with green wavelengths, "your order will be ready soon. Would you like to pay with a discount eyeball scan today?"

"NO" we all say loudly in unison, knowing we're seeing with the eyes of freedom.

"Thank you" the orb recites, "The humanish server will be with you shortly. Thank you for dining with us today." The green wavelength disappears and the orb goes dark.

CitiZen Six looks at us in an inquiring way and says "What if you could have ten human souls, free to choose anything and never get a red remark?"

"What would that be like?" I say sarcastically, just thinking of the possibilities but knowing they're impossible.

"Imagine a world of self-understanding, where the devices are external and My Assistant doesn't exist" says CitiZen

Six with deep, hopeful eyes.

"Then how do you know what to do in life?" I ask, wondering what it would be like without technology as part of my core being.

"You just know" CitiZen Six says, without a wink. He breathes in, out, and continues "What you see and hear and feel in everyday life is just an illusion, you're aware of that already."

"Yes, we're aware" Daisy says, looking both at him and me. I'm recalling the school, the carousel, the Routine. Daisy is recalling too and we nod our heads in agreement.

"Yes, good. But did you know," CitiZen Six says, "Behind the illusion is reality?"

"What reality?" I say sharply remembering my own thoughts from my own mind from the forrest to the stream, from twilight in the valley to dread in the tower.

"The reality that we're in this moment, of course" CitiZen Six says and continues "Look. Whatever led to this moment, and what happens now is a new testament to freedom."

Hmmm, I know the new testament is part of the Ban the Bad Feelings set of books, but also the talk of freedom without qualification. What is he hinting at.

"So when you think of, say, a banned book, an unhealthy drink, a revolutionary party, you'll feel shame or guilt because the perfectionism gene has been inserted into your memeories. These are passed as thoughts through a virtual mirror, which reflects the Aithority's version of reality.

"The Virtual Mirror is the device used to trigger specific memeories and through the device guide your thoughts, which guide your actions. You might take flight into the temporary enjoyments of life and then you're red remarked. The fear of red remarks is controlling your mind. But when you're free from the mainnet you know what it's truly like to be human."

"And what's it like to be human, since you were made to be perfect?" I say sarcastically, thinking he's got these kind of knowitall genes protruding out of his fame.

"It might surprise you that all us so-called Magnificent

Ten weren't engineered to be perfect. We weren't engineered at all."

Moment of silence. Wait. Stunned.

Just then the drinks come by a humanish waiteress. We sit and look at the drinks for a few seconds. Tik tok. The waiteress leaves. We say thank you and look at CitiZen Six.

CitiZen Six explains "The Magnificent was an artificial story from the dominant script. I don't have any special genes, just the ones my mamy and papy gave me."

"Seriousishly?" I say, looking at his big body, considering my own engineered frailty and his natural manish strength. How is that real!?

"Another A game" Daisy says. "Control the masses with fear but keep a few free to use as lab rats. Bruh."

"Yes, Daisy, excellent. And then?" CitiZen Six asks.

I regain my attention, jump in and say "And then you get to do whatever you want, and your moves help the system predict what others would do without artificial genetics."

"You've got it They. Predictions generate the sense of order, or at least the illusion of a familiar, ordered world. We're basically a test sample. And never forget" CitiZen Six says, looking at us with firm intent, "the results of our little experiment in freedom will be used to uphold the system through the guise of order."

"To keep things AS is" Daisy says.

"You're AS right" CitiZen Six says.

I interrupt. "Wait a second. So the system just takes care of you, like without you submitting brain waves or working?" I ask smartish, because without the technology how could anyone function. And with his inheritance he's got it pretty easy.

CitiZen Six doesn't look as stunned as I wanted him to, he's more calm. Doesn't respond. He acts as if we weren't listening. "No more new information today. It's time to form a party" he says and lifts his glass slowly to take a drink.

"So, Cheers" Daisy says, feeling the awkward moment, "to the revolutionary party."

"To the revolutionary party!" we say, and lift our glasses, not knowing what each other's eyes were telling. But feeling our hearts beat together as we create a new world.

Just then the first people arrive, wearing their singlasses, jumping around with energy, ready for the after party.

CitiZen Six calls to the Table Orb, "Orb, bring the humanish manager to our table."

"Is there something I can help you with before calling on the Restauranteur?" The orb says.

"No, dear" CitiZen Six says, "Just bring the Restauranteur."

"They will be at your table shortly" the orb says and goes dark again.

The other Doers sit around at other tables chatting. They see us and we see them. We slightly nod and they nod back. Singlasses, artificial prom clothes, sugary drinks, no red remarks. We all share the determination of freedom within and the tech without.

The Zentran teens sit, chatting amongst themselves, laughing without fear of red remarks or judgements from Zentra peers, parents and the like. And now others come in, the DeZentra crowd of teens. Not from the prom, but wearing what appears to be singlasses.

Now with tables full, the Restauranteur comes out of the back and directly to our table. They're a They! Transhuman adult, professional, kindish looking, just a regular humanish.

"Good evening," they says, "How can I help you?"

"Hi" Citizen Six says and takes off his singlasses, looking eye to eye with the humanish, as if they met before.

"Did you hear about the after party?" he asks.

"Yes, yes I did" the Restauranteur says, "and instructions received. The spot is free for you to use, just make sure everyone speaks easy. I assume you'll arrange the arrangements. See you later, Six" they says, looks at us briefly, twists their hips, winks, and struts away in theyfashion.

CitiZen Six looks at us as the place gets louder. He puts his singlasses back on. "You've got balls?" he says to me.

"I don't know" I answer, wondering if it's a literal question.

"Yeah, you got em" CitiZen Six says, "the biggest balls of them all."

I don't know what he means. I'm a nongenitaled They transhuman, born of a byte meme, unlike this beautifully unique zygoat of a man.

"You know what I'm talking about" CitiZen Six says. "From the chem lab."

"What are you talking about?" I say, acting confused, hoping he's onto something else. I'm hiding the truth and feeling the marbles in my pocket just to double check they're there.

"Those are the payment" CitiZen Six continues. "Taking Zentra balls was ballsy" he smirks, and says "You could trade those balls anywhere around here. The restaurant will trade a whole night of party for up to 100 in a privy room with unshared memories at no extra cost. Everything is arranged."

"Memeories" I say, making sure he gets it right.

CitiZen Six looks at me strangely.

"He meant what he said, They" Daisy says and looks at him, both through and between glasses, "Memories."

"Memories" says CitiZen Six, "Not data. These you keep to yourself."

"Woah" I say. "But what about tomorrow? Will I have my own memories then? Will you be there to help us? What will we tell my Assistant?"

"Nothing. My Assistant is nothing, do you hear me. Nothing but a machine. I do have some bad news. We hacked the central processor and found out tomorrow you will be kicked out of the Alcademy for this party and stealing the balls, and this may be the last time you see me. Take care They.

"And Daisy, the Cobra's yours. Keep her on the road next time."

He gulps his drink down and gets up to leave.

"What about me tomorrow? Will They and I be

separated?" Daisy asks. I wonder what she's getting at.

"Remember escaping the Identity Police? Ghosts? You're gone too. Time to find or found a new school and friends. You both have no choice but to party on."

"Thanks CitiZen Six" Daisy says, "I have the BitoCode, do you think Tenka Bito's DeZen Coin would help us start over?"

"Go ahead and give the code to me. The Collective Mind can use zero knowledge to prove if the code is authentic without revealing its secrets."

Daisy realizes she doesn't have it nor does her dress have pockets nor is it in her small bag, where once spaghetti and the BitoCode filled the now empty space.

"I see you've changed your clothes since we first met" CitiZen Six says to Daisy, "maybe the code was...in your jeans?"

"Tsilekwa!" Daisy shaits, then calms down her voice. But her rage is still apparent with heavy breathing.

"The dressing room" she says but I already knew. Could have also been in the embarrassing shower underneath Aithority Tower, or when using the spaghetti on the daemon dogs. The BitoCode could even be in the cyberdump by now or sold for some pizzas.

"Well, the good news is the Collective Mind has given you some DeZen tokens, to help you get started in new schools and live beyond the Routine."

CitiZen Six then pulls a fine cloth out of his jacket. He unfolds and shows it to us in a double helix movement. The cloth reads "Liebestraum." Love dream my heart tells me. He takes the cloth, softly lays it on top of the table orb, covering the whole orb. He then pulls out and touches his finger to the cloth, finely balancing it on top of the globe, nods cheers to anyone wishing him adieu, and the gentlish leave the building.

The Restauranteur appears and motions us over. We leave the cloth and go to the Restauranteur.

They look at me and I at they. I reach into my pocket and grab the balls, magnetically clinging to each other. I know these balls contain memeories and possibly the cure to thought viruses. But I hand them the balls, they take them, and they say "Use the code word to Speak Easy" then motion us behind the curtain.

There we come upon the kitchen on one side with bustling humanoid and humanish cooks, and on the other a cleaning closet. We open the door to the cleaning closet. It's very humanish with a broom, mop bucket, pail, rags, and cleaning liquid. It smells a bit like trash in here.

"Liebestraum" Daisy says aloud. She knew. The back wall pops open slightly, reveals itself as a door. We push it open and enter a spiral staircase and go up. We reach the door and knock three times. The door opens up and we're suddenly on a large rooftop terrace. There's cool beats in the background, a humanish bartender, some chill areas and a large dance floor overlooking the water.

No caimeras. No hidden maics. No gadgets. No sensors. No internal relay. No brains. Set.

Daisy runs over to the edge, pulling me with her by the hand. "Look out there" she says. "Endless."

"Endless" I say, enjoying this moment of life with her in the dark of the night, stars up above, water below, heart beating inside. Me and her. Endless. Like under the bleachers but in this moment, not hiding, just free.

She lifts her shades and I lift mine. We take one more deep long look at each other and kiss. We don't know if this is the last time so we do our best. Tomorrow never comes. Carpe Diem, to use a Ban the Bad word. I enjoy this moment with all my heart, my soul, my energy, my strength.

We stop kissing once the others come loudly through the door. Happy to see everyone. So much diversity, five, ten, twenty, even thirty people in singlasses come out of the closet and onto the large dance floor.

We see Jonny Pockets, White Hair and some Cypherpunks enter. Immigrants, Settlers, Natives, and everything between. Zentrans and DeZentrans. Even though our genes and our minds are semi-controlled by some insane regime, and we know our deathish fate, our spirit is free. I'm ready to die for a big open party.

"Ready to live, wormbrain?" Daisy says and smiles her endless smile. I nod, and she goes over to the dance floor and starts movin' and shakin' to the oldies with the others.

I put back on my shades and look again out into the distance. Far away I can barely make out the lighthouse and a light out to sea. I look more closely, watching its light sway back and forth in perfect motion.

As I'm about to turn around and join Daisy to dance the night away - before going home, crashing, and figuring out my new life in this brave weird world - the lighthouse shines in my direction.

For a moment, a split second, the light beam goes off course and straight to me; flashing once, then turning back to the sea. The waves roar. The birds fly across the moon.

A meme pops into my head. My heart sinks. The flash appears through my singlasses. Bright. Blinding. Light. I see the words pass by my eyes. Three words, third time today. I won't tell Daisy. But the flash was clear.

the Aithority knows.

www.ingramcontent.com/pod-product-compliance
Lightning Source LLC
Chambersburg PA
CBHW020421180626
46812CB00003B/1081